VAMPIRE KING

ZARA NOVAK

OLIVIA

As soon as I stepped off the train, I could tell I was in danger. This city had a reputation, one that didn't exactly inspire confidence or feelings of safety for a small girl like me. Any girl in her right mind would have turned this job down when it fell on her desk, but not me. I wasn't sure if I was an idiot, arrogant, or just a glutton for punishment. The truth was I was after a challenge, and a trip to Carcoza city was certainly that.

"Olivia?" a woman said from further down the platform. "Olivia Brown? It's Victoria, Victoria Dunn. I'm your contact."

I let out a grateful breath, some of my anxiety receding as I walked towards the contact, the one the agency promised would be here to meet me when I arrived. She was in her fifties, tall, slender, with bright silver hair pulled back in a professional up do. "I knew it was you. I recognized you from the cover."

"Cover?" I asked as I shook her hand. The smartly dressed woman opened her large clutch and pulled out a copy of my book, holding it up as if to prove a point. I cringed inwardly at the sight of the thing, hoping she'd put it away sooner than later. Blazoned in bold white across the cover was the words *Opened: Dissecting the Minds of Ameri-*

ca's *Most Dangerous Criminals*. Above those words was my photo, accompanied by name in all caps at the bottom.

Dr. Olivia R. Brown.

It was weird, but I had never felt proud of the doctorate title, it always made me feel old, even though I still a few years shy of thirty. I guess in a way it just felt too formal for me.

"Ah, I see," I said as the woman slid the book back into her bag. When the agency told me someone would meet me here at the platform, I hadn't expected a fan.

"Sorry, I know it's unprofessional," she laughed. "But I've been following your career for several years, ever since you began actually. You're practically a rock star in the CIA."

"I didn't know the CIA were such big fans of clinical psychiatry," I mused.

"We're a small department, but we're growing rapidly. Uh, please, follow me. We'll talk as we walk." Victoria looked over my shoulder and pulled me into a quick walk with her. Looking back I saw a group of unsettling men lurking in the shadows off from the edge of the platform. A chill trickled down my spine.

Carcoza city. A festering pot of violent crime.

My mind couldn't help flickering through the stats I had unhelpfully memorized on the way over here. In the last few decades Carcoza had exploded in population. Starting as a small gambling town in the middle of the desert, it quickly became an untamed breeding ground of sin, growing in size and stature so rapidly that it dwarfed its older sister, Las Vegas, which was only a few hours away on the mag-train.

It was hard to believe that a hundred million people now lived here, but looking at the skyline on the approach, I could start to believe it. An untold number of skyscrapers, dark and black, filling the horizon as far as the eye could see.

Tens of thousands of murders. Thousands more people missing. An untold number of rapes and abductions. Crime rate through the roof. Why did I come here again?

Victoria walked quickly, her feet falling with purpose and direction. It was the air of a woman that was used to walking through dangerous areas. Move fast. Keep your head down. Don't make eye contact.

I hurried beside her, trying to stay as close as I could.

We headed up a set of tall black stairs that opened into a large and bustling station building, filled with thousands of people all hurrying in different directions under the tall and vaulted gothic ceilings. On a wall ahead of us hundreds of giant holographic boards projected information about the latest arrivals and departures.

"Stay close!" Victoria shouted over the din. "And keep a tight hold of your bags!"

I followed her through the crowds, my heart beating in my chest as we cut across the room. Within a minute we had crossed the throng and found ourselves on an escalator that was heading down.

"I suppose it would be really unprofessional to ask for an autograph?" she joked.

"Uh, sure. When we get in the car."

I had to admit that still felt weird too. Celebrity brought a strange kind of attention, one that I was never sure I would get used to. I'd done a few book signings now and readings at the behest of my agent, my publisher, and contractual obligations, but if I had my way, I'd rather stay out of the limelight altogether.

When I published my book, I never expected I would receive the kind of attention that I have. Things just exploded overnight and now I found myself as a minor celebrity, the 'Superstar Psychiatrist' that can get the deepest darkest criminals to divulge their secrets.

Victoria laughed nervously at her request. "Sorry, I'm usually a lot more reserved than this, but I really admire your work. Just how do you do it? Getting those men to confess to all those new cases?"

It's a question I'd been asked many times. The answer was basically rehearsed by now. "Just listening and talking. I push, they pull away. I back off, they open up. It requires patience and feeling. The one thing you have to remember is that these men want to talk. They want the attention." Victoria nodded as though she completely agreed.

"Well I've read the transcripts; I have to say your approach is remarkable. Right from the offset. You've never put a foot out of line. Even with Jack Carrington." A cold shiver came over Victoria. "Talk about jumping in at the deep end. You handled it so well, for someone so young as well."

"I got lucky, but yes, Jack opened a lot of doors for me."

During college I'd written to a number of ultraviolent prisoners, asking if they'd like to be part of a study for my degree. Most didn't respond, but I got lucky with one, *Candy Jack,* a serial killer from the southwest that butchered dozens of women. Jack had been incarcerated fifteen years earlier for the rape and abduction of fifteen women, and was suspected of another thirty, but the police had never been able to find the evidence.

"But for him to open up after all that time," Victoria said. "Amazing really. You seem to get into people's minds. "You seem to... have a gift." She looked over at me briefly as we carried on through the station, an exit for the street looming just ahead. I made eye contact for a second and decided to get a read on her.

In a flash her emotional state came through to me, a collection of bright colors and shapes projected at the front of her mind, giving me a glimpse into her thoughts and feelings. I had half-wondered if there was jealousy or contempt hinging behind her words but looking inside I could see Victoria was genuinely enthusiastic, and inspired by my track record so far.

The truth was that I'd always had this ability to read people. I wasn't quite sure what it was, and I didn't know how to explain it other than intuition, but I always knew I might be able to use this power for good.

And I did.

It started that day when I went to visit the serial killer Candy Jack. I was nervous as hell going in, and as soon as I set through that door and sat down at the table across from him, I could feel the dark depravity rolling right off him. The things he wanted to do to me. The rushes and surges of rage and arousal. Something was missing, something that meant he wasn't all there.

But I noticed there was weakness in him, it happened when we were talking about his upbringing. Mentioning his mother inspired rage, but when I mentioned his grandmother, I felt a flash of something, a trace of human warmth that I hadn't seen in him yet.

Latching onto that warmth, I knew I could use it to open him up. Within forty minutes of me walking through that door I had the infamous *Candy Jack* blubbering in tears, writing down the locations of thirty Jane Does as fast as he could.

Telepathy is the wrong word, because I cannot see people's thoughts or even guess what they're thinking, but for some reason their emotional state comes through to me, and with those puzzle pieces I can just about shift any conversation in any direction.

Getting Jack to open up basically shot me to fame overnight. After that the DOJ hired me for a summer internship and threw a stack of manilla folders on my desk. I spent that summer touring across the country and visiting more killers with links to cold cases. A string of successes proved my initial win with Jack wasn't a lucky fluke. By September of that year I'd pried another 8 confessions and pulled up evidence to solve another 25 cold cases.

Now I had a level of fame, and for some reason killers still wanted to talk to me. I guess they saw it as some sort of challenge. The truth of the matter is that I could get secrets, if they had them.

That brief glimpse of Victoria, it told me she was hiding something too. Something colossal.

I trust her though. But she feels sick. Sick with nerves.

The station opened into a bustling sidewalk and for the first time I got a glimpse of Carcoza from the street level. Victoria approached a sleek black car that waited directly ahead and opened the door. She gestured for me to climb in and I did.

She climbed in and closed the door, the driver setting off without a word being spoken between them. Victoria pressed a button and a glass partition slid up, separating the back of the car from the front. Then she pulled something out of her bag, it was about the size and length of a pen, but a little thicker. It was a little chrome cylinder with a blue glass orb on the top. There was one solitary black button about halfway up the cylinder.

"What on earth is that?" I asked, keeping myself in tune with her emotional state now. She wouldn't know I was reading her, no one knew about my ability, I'd never admitted as much out loud. She was extremely nervous, and I could tell she was in a situation she didn't want to be in. It felt like she was about to offer me a choice, and perhaps tell me this secret she was hiding.

"How long have you worked for the DOJ now?" she asked.

"Four years. Just shy."

She nodded. "I see. Well. How much do you know about Carcoza?"

I laughed and looked out the window at the sea of skyscrapers stretching in every direction. The city had a dark and malignant beauty, a crown of opulence and wealth that stretched high above my head in every direction, but just glancing at the street level was sign enough that poverty existed here too. Rampant homelessness, sidewalks packed with beggars, sex workers. Thousands of crimes happening every day, maybe even every minute.

"I'm not sure I'd stay here long."

A wash of warmth flurried through her at my joke. I wanted her to relax a little. Whatever was eating her up, it wasn't good.

"I felt the same when I first came here. The truth is that... well..." She looked away, holding back whatever it was she was about to say. I felt her direction shift. "The agency I represent has taken an interest in your abilities. To say your track record is anything less than remarkable would be an insult."

"Thanks?"

"I'm about to share something with you. Something about the city, and its inhabitants. You probably won't believe me. It's fine. I didn't believe it first myself either, but we're at a crossroads now."

"What is it?" I asked, prompting her after another long silence. She drew in a very long breath.

"Miss Brown, do you believe in vampires?"

I stared blankly at her for a good few seconds and then burst out laughing. "I'm sorry, what?"

"Vampires. As in—"

"Pale figures, dark hair, pointy fangs? Dracula?"

"Yes. Exactly."

"Uh, no. I don't." I vaguely remembered reading something about vampire cults in Carcoza but had merely brushed it off as just that—a cult. "Do you?" I asked cautiously.

"I don't believe in them. I don't have to. I already know they are real." She looked me in the eye this time, her face and emotional state betraying no sign that this was a joke. I could tell that she meant the words with absolute sincerity. Underneath that sincerity was a slight feeling of embarrassment, as though she didn't even want to have this conversation, there was also impatience, proving that she'd had this conversation before with others and just wanted to get it over with and for me to accept it.

"You're telling the truth," I said in realization.

"I hoped you of all people would see that."

"And what is that in your hand?" I gestured the unusual metallic cylinder.

"This will erase your mind of the last minute. A cautionary device. Sometimes necessary when pulling back the curtain and showing people the real world. Something told me I wouldn't need it with you, but... you never know."

Victoria slipped the device back into her bag and zipped it up.

"I'm sorry, a mind blanking device? That doesn't exist."

"Just like vampires?" she said with a raised brow. Once again, a glimpse of her mental state told me she was being absolutely genuine. Furthermore I got no impression that she was mentally ill, which was important, because people were able to believe themselves and still be mentally deluded.

"Okay, say I believe you. What now then?"

"Well I say congratulations, you got the job. If you want it of course."

"I didn't realize this was a job offer, I thought this was a one off, talking to some inmates and getting information."

"That's exactly what it is, but you won't get in without my approval, and that involves learning the secret."

"That vampires exist?" She nodded her head lightly. "How do you even know I believe you? For all you know I'm just humoring you."

"You strike me as the type of woman that doesn't waste other people's time. Your work is evidence enough of that. Whether or not you believe it doesn't matter to me, but I encourage you strongly to believe what I'm saying. The man you're going to interview, or should I say, the *vampire*, he is an extremely dangerous individual, and he will shred you to pieces if he finds an ounce of vulnerability."

I stared into Victoria's eyes, wondering for the first time in my life if I had found someone that could circle my abilities and use them against me as a joke. As I read her state though I realized fully that she wasn't joking, and she was completely serious. Not only serious, but nervous about the destination that lay ahead.

My abilities to read peoples' emotions has a lot of advantages, but I must say the one drawback is that I feel a trace amount of whatever emotion I'm reading, good or bad. Right now Victoria was racked with nerves, which struck me as odd because she seemed like a hardy woman.

"Why are you so nervous?" I said to her. "You're making me nervous too." She couldn't know I was feeling her emotion, it wasn't unusual for normal people to mirror the feelings of those around them though.

Victoria pointed at a large black building that loomed ahead, locked behind impossibly high walls and tall metal fencing. "Carcoza prison," she said. "One of the most dangerous places on earth. Your subject is in there."

"Who is he?" I asked, my throat suddenly dry. Our car stopped at a fenced gate, which opened after the driver produced a badge. We drove on through, the gates closing behind us. Up ahead the building stood large, perhaps twenty floors tall, blocking out the sun from the sky.

Victoria handed me a photo of a man with deathly pale skin, short black hair and eyes that almost looked... *red?* If I didn't have the vague idea this man was some dangerous and violent criminal, I would almost be tempted to say he was attractive, because he was.

A strong masculine jaw, perfect bone structure, piercing eyes that seemed to leap up off the page and cut me in two.

"Lucas Vancino," she answered, her eyes concentrating on something outside. "The most dangerous vampire in this entire god forsaken city."

"Vancino?" I said, my hands trembling for some reason as I held the photo. I don't know what it was, but just looking at the man undid me. I quickly put the photo into my pocket and steadied myself, trying to keep the reaction hidden from Victoria.

2

LUCAS

The walls are whispering again, and they aren't saying pretty things. Day 3458. Nearly ten years of my life gone for a crime I didn't commit.

When I woke up this morning, I could feel a strange energy in the air, the walls of my cells buzzing with a keen vibration, the entire prison almost trembling with the threat of something new.

I already know what's coming because of my connections in here. Even though I'm kept in complete isolation permanently, I have my ways of talking to other inmates. Something very big is coming today, and it's not going to be pretty. Still, it might be a chance for me to get out, and I might just have to jump on that train.

God knows they're not going to let me out of here otherwise.

My cell is decidedly spacious. I suppose you could say I have the penthouse of the prison. My cage is set directly in the middle of a larger room, and inside that cage I spend the majority of my days. I have a bed, a toilet and sink, a shower that comes on for ten minutes every morning and night—freezing cold water of course.

Outside the cage there is twenty feet of empty floor up until the walls. On one wall there is a two-way mirror, and next to that mirror is the only door out of here. It's barred, solid iron and at least three feet thick.

There are actually two layers to my cage. The first features conventional iron bars. There are 243 of them—you have a lot of time to count on the inside—and I can bend them quite freely with my strength if I want to, and I have.

Since then they installed another layer of bars surrounding that first layer. This second layer is made of silver, and the bars are arranged in a way that they are a lattice of crucifixes. If that wasn't enough to keep me back—it was—a powerful electrical charge runs through the silver, strong enough to knock me back and put me out for a few minutes—I know, I have tried that too.

They want to keep me in complete isolation. They want me to go mad, they want me to take the fall for something I didn't do, but I'll hold on hope. I know that one day I'll get out, and I'll get my revenge. My captors don't even give me the luxury of books, so I have to occupy myself by keeping fit and training. With my legs hooked over the bars on the ceiling of my cell I finish my morning with sit up 605.

That's when Herb came in. My guard. My connection to the outside. Herb doesn't know it, but he's the one that lets me know what's happening.

"Morning Herb," I said, dropping down onto the ground in the middle of my cell.

"Vancino," Herb said in response. He walked over to my cell and placed my food tray on the floor, pushing it over with a long pole, making sure that no one ever gets within fifteen feet of me. The tray slid under a gap in the cell. I took the jug of blood and pushed the tray back.

"Thanks Herb. Say. What time is it now?"

It's taken a longtime, but I've managed to set up a system with Herb. For a few microseconds I can hypnotize him and swap a sentence or two of cryptic communication with the other prisoners in here. The cameras that constantly record my cell from all angles haven't picked up on my trick so far.

Herb's eyes flashed white for a second and he gave the answer.

"Oh, it's uh ten," he said, even looking at his watch. That wasn't the time of course, he was reading back another answer that I had programmed him for.

"I think your watch might be out of sync there herb. It's probably closer to half nine."

"Huh?" The spell ended with my release, and Herb looked at me. "What did you say Vancino?"

"What time is it?" I asked again, asking for real this time.

"It's half nine, Vancino, and you god damn know it. Breakfast at half nine every day. See you in three hours."

"Not likely," I muttered.

Herb turned to leave but stopped before reaching the door. "Oh, Vancino, you have a visitor today."

My entire body suddenly froze. "What? What did you just say?"

"A visitor. Someone to see you."

"I'm not allowed visitors," I said, merely repeating the rules they had put down for me and me alone.

"Well, looks like you've got one today. Some doctor bitch. They're going to make you talk. You'll give up your secrets, you sick bastard."

With that Herb left, the solid iron door clanging shut behind him. That last part of the conversation was completely unexpected. It wasn't a secret code sent through hypnotized messages, Herb was being genuine. Someone was coming to visit me. How interesting.

Taking my jar of blood I sat down on the bed and drank it all down slowly, reflecting on the conversation I'd just had with Herb in secret. What I'd essentially said to him boiled down to this:

Hey, Herb. What time's the jailbreak today?

10am – answer courteous of my friend Gonzola in the cell down the hall. We used Herb to pass very short messages between one another.

But even without Gonzola and my cryptic messages anyone could guess something was coming this morning. You can always feel it in a prison, it's like the air is vibrating with the threat of violence.

The prisoners have been planning this riot for a longtime, and it's going to be huge. It's also going to be my ticket out of here.

I think my shrink might just have to wait.

Not long after a light that above the shower illuminated, letting me know that the water would run for the next five minutes. With my workout done I stripped down and turned on the shower, bracing myself as I stepped underneath the freezing cold water. I'd gotten quite used to these ice cold showers now, they even helped wake me up.

I washed myself quickly from head to toe, removing the grime and sweat that worked up from my constant workouts. With a few minutes remaining until the water shut off, I simply stood there with my eyes closed and my jaw tensed, forcing myself to stay underneath the ice cold water.

Don't get out. Don't give in. Stay strong.

The light overhead went off and the water ended without warning. I toweled off, put on my prison-approved underwear and boilersuit, and sat on my bed. Time didn't mean much in here, especially as I wasn't allowed a clock or any means of tracking the hours, but I'd gotten very good at tracking the passage of time mentally, and I knew there was only fifteen minutes until the riot would begin.

I was clean, well-rested, fed, and ready for the inevitable chaos that was about to come my way. Nothing was going to throw a wrench in the works this morning.

But then the heavy iron door on the exterior wall opened. A guard stepped in and behind him was the most beautiful woman I had seen in my life, a young girl, maybe in her mid-twenties, with chestnut brown hair, eyes a guy could fall into, and a figure that immediately made me to stand attention.

"Stand up Vancino," the guard ordered. "In the middle of your cell."

I took note of the electro-prod in his hand and followed suit. The guards didn't like to get too close if they could help it, and they'd come up with this special long-distance taser purely to deal with me. I had to give it to them, the damned thing hurt.

"What's this?" I said, speaking to the guard, but not taking my eyes off the girl at all.

"I present to you inmate 1833446," the guard said to the girl, ignoring me completely. "Lucas Vancino. You have one hour." He moved to leave but then stopped. "I strongly encourage you don't pass the line painted on the floor." He pointed to a blue line painted around the perimeter of my cell, halfway between the outer crucifix cage and the wall with the iron door.

"Why?" she said to the guard.

"He's… resourceful," was all the guard said. "Knock on the door if you want to leave."

With that he turned and left, the heavy iron door clanging shut behind him. The girl watched him leave, stared at the closed door for a moment and then very slowly looked back at me. Right away I could sense fear and intrigue, two oceans of thought clashing against one another, creating a maelstrom of curiosity and desire within her. My senses hyper-focused, I heard her swallow down her nerves. I felt her heart beating in her chest, even though she was a good fifteen feet away from me.

I wasn't sure if it was the fact that I had been alone for almost ten years, or if this really was the most beautiful woman I'd seen in my entire life, either way, I didn't know what to do with myself. I was a mess.

On the inside anyway. On the outside I tried to maintain an aura of indifference and intimidation. I could tell she was waiting for me to say something. I could very well play the waiting game and see what she said first, but that felt… rude.

"Welcome. What is your name?"

"Olivia. Olivia Brown."

"You're a shrink?"

She shook her head, the light moving over the delicate features of that perfect face. "A clinical psychiatrist."

"Sounds like another word for shrink."

"Shrinks fix people. That's not what I'm here to do."

I laughed. I had to admire her honesty. "So what does a clinical psychiatrist do then?"

"Normally they fix people too, so I guess I'm splitting hairs a little.

But in my area of expertise, I practice my work a little differently. They sent me here to get information out of you."

"I see," I said. "Well, there's a wall right behind you. Feel free to bang your head against it. I assure you the experience will be very similar."

The hint of a smile curled on those perfect pink lips. It did something to me. It filled with me something I'd never felt before. Fuck. I could stare at that smile for the rest of my life.

"You don't want to talk?" she asked, framing the question in an innocuous way.

"I've done nothing but talk since I got here. No one listens. What exactly is it you want to know?"

She took a few steps forward, stopping just short of the blue line on the ground. The perimeter represented the outer reach of my vampiric intention, my ability to take over people's minds and move them against their will.

"I'm basically a psychological interrogator. I prey on your weaknesses and get you to confess to whatever secrets you might be hiding."

Once again, I found myself taken aback by her brazen honesty. "You know if this was a game of poker you basically just told me your hand."

"It doesn't really matter," she said with an air of indifference. "The fact is that I'm good, and I have a track record of one hundred percent."

"And how many men have you got to confess?"

"So far? I've done just over fifteen cases, and everyone has ended with success."

Consider me intrigued. "Well then, I'm very excited to see what you have to say, but there's just one little hitch. I'm a little busy this morning."

She laughed and rolled her eyes, crossing her arms and shifting her weight onto one hip, in a way that said *fuck off buddy.* "Is that so? Is there a lot going on in solitary confinement this morning?"

In my head I knew there were only ten minutes until the walls holding this prison together were going to start tumbling down. "Listen darling. I really think it's for the best that you get out of here. Far away from here. As fast as you possibly can. I'm talking… minutes here."

I felt something tickle the back of my neck then, like fingers tapping gently on the skin. Looking into her eyes I realized this girl was reading me somehow, and as her expression changed, I saw she believed my warning.

"You're telling the truth," she said. "You really believe that I'm in mortal danger."

"Wouldn't say it otherwise."

"From what? You?"

"Little lady I'm certainly trouble, but the only kind of grief I'd give you is the bad kind."

"Meaning?"

"Step across that line and find out."

She looked down at the line as though she was considering it but didn't move any closer. "If you don't mind, I'd like to start with a few questions about your childhood—"

"Perhaps you misheard me," I interrupted. "You need to get the hell out of here now before you get hurt. Something bad is going to happen, and this isn't the place for a small defenseless girl."

"And why do you care so much?"

"What?"

"What does it matter to you? Why the consideration? I'm just a stranger to you, and given your track record…" She opened the file in her hands and flicked through it quickly. "The value of human life is something that you don't give much thought to."

Truth told I didn't know why I was so concerned about the annoying little shrink, or whatever it was she wanted to call herself. All I knew is that all hell was going to break loose in a few minutes, and I felt sick to the stomach with the thought of her getting hurt. There were real animals in here, and they wouldn't hesitate to destroy something beautiful.

The most annoying thing is that I'd somehow given her a lead in our little back and forth. I wanted something from her—to get out and protect herself—and she was fully in her power to use that against me to get what she wanted. It was just a question of whether she realized it or not.

"Tell you what," she said. "Let's strike a bargain." *Fuck. She realized.* "You answer my questions and I'll get out of here. Then we both get what we want. Sound good?"

I grinded my jaw, unable to help smiling as I stared into the eyes of this master interrogator, whoever she was. If I didn't know any better, I'd say she was reading my every thought, which was impossible, because she was human.

"Deal. Hurry up and fire away."

"Why did you kill them? The two hundred women found in the freight containers on the dock?"

"I didn't I was set up. It was—" I froze, stopping myself from saying the one thing I couldn't say. "It wasn't me."

"Something you've maintained all these years. You claim to know who's responsible, but won't give a name, why?" I stared at her in silence, my lack of an answer being answer enough, if she was smart enough to figure it out. "I see," she said after a long moment. "What about the evidence at the scene? The fingerprints? The surveillance footage? You were arrested at the docks, trying to flee the scene."

The real answer: an incredibly sophisticated set up. Why was I at the scene? Because I was trying to save those women. Where did the evidence come from? Clever fabrication. Who was responsible? Fats Manucci and his organized crime family.

"Are we done here?" I said.

"You didn't answer my questions. I need a confession. If you want me to go."

I let out a deep and long sigh, counting down the remaining minutes in my head. Truth told I wasn't sure the little chestnut-haired doctor could get out now if she wanted to. I might just have to take matters into my own hands.

"Let me turn this session on its head for a moment. How is it you can see inside my mind?" The question caught her off guard, forcing her to do a doubletake.

"Excuse me?" An awkward laugh betrayed her surprise.

"You've been one step ahead of me for this entire conversation, somehow. Five minutes you've been in here, and already you've figured out more than anyone else ever has. I'll give it to you, you're good. The thing is that you know the answer, but you're dancing around it for some reason, so I gotta ask, why?"

The shrink faltered, her mouth opening and closing again as she scrambled for an answer. "Because—"

"I'll tell you why," I said. "Because you know that I'm innocent, and furthermore you know that my captors know that too. So you're trying to silently reconcile that fact while also asking yourself why 'the good guys' would deliberately keep an innocent man in solitary confinement for almost ten years of his life."

"Because you know something," she said. "You have something on them."

"Bingo. And if anything happens to me, it gets out."

"So why wait here?"

"Because—" Because… I couldn't say that part out loud. It went against the deal. My captors and I were in a stalemate. I stay inside and do my time. Innocent people don't get hurt. "You already know that too," I said, looking into her eyes as I felt that phantom touch tapping over the back of my neck. "Just who the hell are you? How can you read me like this?"

The doctor swallowed, realizing that I had figured her out completely. "I think our conversation is done. I should leave."

"Your time to leave with safety has passed," I said. "I'm afraid you're in my hands now." I counted down the seconds in my head, knowing full-well what was going to happen when ten came around. "What time is it?" I asked.

She glanced down at her watch. "9:59."

"Here's what's going to happen. You're going to stay close and do as I say. It's the only way we both get out of here alive. Got that?"

Suddenly a giant slamming sound rumbled through the facility. It was the distant sound of an explosion. Dust rained down from my cell ceiling and I felt the explosion rumble through the floor. The lights flickered out for a second and then the emergency lighting came on.

"What was that?" the shrink asked. I moved forward and tore open the bars of my cell, grimacing as I ripped through the silver crucifix lattice too. The metal and the symbols burned like hell, but I couldn't let that stop me now. With the power down I could stomach the pain, get out of this cell and get the little shrink to safety.

She stood motionless, watching in terror as the giant vampire prisoner ripped through the one thing keeping me from her. I very casually stepped out of the cell, my skin hissing and steaming as it healed from the silver burns. A few paces later I reached her, my skin almost fully healed, my giant form looming over her tiny body.

"W-What's happening?!" she stammered.

I picked up the tiny brunette and threw her over my shoulder. "Jailbreak darling."

3

OLIVIA

*P*ossession, control, dominance—all of it roiling through this brute as a whirlwind of fire, pushing him to protect me at all costs.

"Hey!" I shouted as he picked me up. "Just what the hell do you think you're doing?! Put me down! Put me down! Guards! Guards!" The huge vampire picked me up with little trouble at all, slinging me over his shoulder like a caveman taking a prize back to his den. I slapped his back as hard as I could and tried to kick, but my blows glanced off his rock hard body like water off a duck's back.

All around I heard commotion erupt through the prison, the sound of muted explosions and gunfire beginning to erupt throughout the facility. I heard men screaming and shouting, alarms began to blare, filling my ears with and endless caterwaul of din.

"Hey!" I shouted again, struggling to make myself heard over the high-pitched wailing. "Put me down!" Vancino took no notice and walked confidently towards the heavy iron door, the only exit leading out of his solitary confinement. He simply waited there for a few seconds, like a big cat waiting to pounce.

"They're going to kill you!" I shouted. "The guards will kill you!"

"The guards are already dead, or will be very shortly," he said back. "Now shut up."

All of a sudden, a wave of gunfire smashed through the one-way mirror looking into the room. The reflective wall shattered into pieces, revealing the room behind it. Lucas was correct about the guards, or he would be in a few seconds at the least. There behind the broken wall of glass I saw numerous inmates fighting with the guards, guns going off in all directions as the two groups fought for control.

I only saw a few seconds of the action before Lucas spun around and threw himself over me, his huge hulking body shielding me as a protective orb. A few seconds later the gunfire in the immediate vicinity stopped and he stood up, slinging me over his shoulder again.

"As promised," a vampire announced from the room behind the shattered mirror. "A way out Vancino. I suggest you move fast if you want to get out of here."

"I appreciate it Gonzola," Lucas said to the vampire. "How bad is it out there?"

"Pretty fucking bad. Say, who's the broad?"

I knew at once the vampire was referring to me. "Who, her? They sent a shrink in. I figured I'd take me a little something to remember my stay here."

The vampire let out a loud laugh, one that echoed around the neighboring din. "Hurry up and get out. I'll have the boys torch the cell, we'll make it look like you didn't get out of here alive. Look for the rabbit."

"Rabbit, got it. Appreciate it. Come see me when you get out. I promise I won't forget this debt."

Suddenly Lucas lunged forward, flying through the observation room and into the hallway outside, the same one I had walked through as Victoria brought me here. Looking around I saw no sign of her anywhere. I barely knew her, but I hoped she had gotten out of here okay. Just before we went through the door Lucas' friend called after him.

"Vancino, take this! You'll need it."

A semi-automatic flew through the air and Lucas caught it effortlessly, thanking his friend before stepping out into the hallway. My view of the events was somewhat limited being thrown over a vampire's shoulder—like some plaything—but the second we stepped into that hallway I was convinced we were going to die.

Alarms blaring, guards screaming, inmates rioting, fires roaring, everywhere I looked the prison was rife with chaos and violence. Lucas stalked through the hallways quickly, lifting his gun and firing at targets I could not see. I managed to glance and saw several other inmates running his way, only to turn around and scramble in the opposite direction when they saw Lucas.

Everyone here is afraid of him.

I didn't have to see that to feel the fear in the air. In general the emotional state of the rioting prison was almost too much to bear, wild men hungry with the prospect of escape and revenge. Rage bleeding through their hearts, violence itching on their closed fists. Lucas somehow navigated the chaos with purpose and focus, a steel ship gliding through a storm of violent madness, pushing all danger out of its way.

It soon became pretty clear that he was moving in the opposite direction of everyone else too, before long we were running down empty hallways. I barely knew the layout of the place because I'd only just got here, but I could swear to god we were moving *into* the prison.

"What are you doing?!" I shouted. "You're going the wrong way!" Even the alarms were in the distance now, and I could finally hear myself screaming at my barbaric captor.

"Are you rooting for me doc?"

"No! I just want to get out of here alive!"

"Trust me then. Those idiots running for the front doors aren't going to find freedom. The only thing waiting for them are the sentry guns on the towers. Luckily you're in the company of a man with inside knowledge."

"You've been in solitary! How can you have inside knowledge?!"

The vampire burst through a pair of doors and we found ourselves in a large mess hall, dead guards, inmates, and shattered glass everywhere. He crossed the room quickly and turned down a side corridor, stopping at a door to a supply closet. He turned me around so I could see and pointed to a very small symbol etched into the wall right at the top near the ceiling. It was a little rabbit head.

"Follow the rabbit," he said.

He opened the door to the supply closet and there at the back was an open sewer grate. Vancino walked straight towards it, placed me on the ground and closed the door behind us. "What now?" I said.

"I jump down. And you follow."

I crossed my arms. "What's to stop me from running away?"

"The other inmates in this prison won't touch you if you're with me. Without me…"

"What?"

"What, you want me to spell it out darling? You'll be raped and dead within twenty minutes. If you're lucky."

Even I didn't have to read his emotions to believe that one. Little as I liked it, my odds in the sewer were far better than going alone. Vancino didn't give me another opportunity to discuss the matter.

His eyes blazed. "Do whatever you like but know this. This sewer is a hundred foot drop, and there's no ladder. I can make it. You can't. I'm going down, and I'll wait exactly thirty seconds. If you don't jump down in that time you've no choice but to turn back and go back out there alone."

He pushed past me and then jumped down, straight into the hole without a second thought. If he was bluffing about the drop my doubts were erased when I heard him hit the distant ground a few seconds later. It was definitely a long drop by the sounds of it.

"Fuck, fuck, fuck," I said to myself quietly, turning around between the sewer entrance and the door as I considered my options. If I was lucky I could get a weapon of sorts to defend myself, find a hiding place and hold out until the guards took control of the prison again. That plan heavily depended on finding a weapon and hiding though. There were still inmates running around, and I only had to cross one to be fresh out of luck.

Rape and death. If you're lucky.

"I can't believe I'm fucking doing this." With a big breath I approached the sewer entrance and tried to steady my nerves. If it hadn't already been thirty seconds, I was certainly getting close. Closing my eyes I stepped forward and plunged down into the dark tunnel, screaming as I fell into the unknown.

Here goes nothing.

My fall came to a stop all of a sudden and I realized I was in Lucas' arms. The large vampire instantly clamped a hand over my mouth, his large barrel chest rising and falling with slow and controlled breaths.

"Quiet," he whispered to me. "Something isn't right here."

Looking around I saw we were in a large underground tunnel; it was dim, spacious, and smelled of damp. The curved ceiling arched high above us, probably about twenty feet, and the walls on our left and right were an equal distance away. It stretched into darkness directly ahead and behind us.

The only light came from torches on the walls, which flickered and danced from whatever gentle breeze moved around down here. It took my eyes a few seconds to adjust, but when they did, I could see the silhouette of a group ahead of us. One of them stepped forward out of the shadow, revealing the face of a pale man with shining red eyes.

"Vancino?" the vampire said, a trace of fear evident on his voice. He was trying to hide his terror, that much I could feel. "What the fuck are you doing here?"

"Gonzola promised me safe passage through these tunnels. We had an arrangement," Lucas said back. Reading Lucas was much simpler because of our proximity, but his thoughts in general signaled a lot clearer than other people. It was a trait I had come to recognize amongst those that were strong of mind and sure of themselves.

The vampire standing further down the tunnel, his thoughts were vague streaks in the darkness. Lucas, his feelings were bright and vivid lines, clear cut patterns with no mistake or doubt. It wasn't really the time to focus on this sort of thing, but that sort of confidence was overwhelmingly attractive.

"No, no. Gonzola paid for one person as well as himself. He said nothing about that one person being Lucas fucking Vancino."

"You got a problem with the name?" Lucas growled.

"Yeah, I do. You're fucking trouble, and a name like that is premium. If the prison finds out I let you through my tunnels, then it's big trouble for me and my boys. Let me cut this short. Fuck off and find another way out."

"Let's cut it even shorter. Turning around isn't an option, so you either let me through or we find trouble."

The vampire standing ahead of us made a small movement of his head, and all of a sudden the group waiting at his rear stepped forward out of the shadow. There had to be twenty of them in total.

"Come on Vancino," the vampire at the front said disparagingly. "Even you can't take this many."

"You sure?" Lucas kept his eye on the group blocking the way, and he didn't budge an inch. I felt a lot of things from the group in front of us, fear mostly, but they were also waiting for a word from their leader, loyal soldiers primed on a hair trigger. Alone I don't think anyone of them would take on Lucas, but with the pressure and security of a group, none would hesitate.

Judging from my reading of Lucas he wasn't too bothered.

A laugh escaped the lead vampire. "Come on Vancino, berserker or not, you ain't got what it takes to handle a group like this. We're not some ragtag street gang. You're talking about Angelo vampire bloodline here. We're strong, we're fast. Just like you."

"You're nothing like me," Vancino said with disinterest. "And I'm not backing down, so I suggest you let me through, or I can start tearing your men apart."

This time more than a few of the men laughed. I had no idea what gave Lucas the confidence to think he could take on twenty opponents at once, but I couldn't fault his concrete self-assurance.

"How about a deal," the leader said. "You give us that pretty little girl you're clinging to, and you can go through."

That suggestion brought about firm feelings of rage within Lucas. He was extremely protective; I just couldn't figure out why.

"How's about this. I keep hold of her and fight you all with one arm. Keep things real fair."

The mediating vampire just shook his head and laughed. "Suit yourself, Vancino. Don't say I didn't try to warn you." He stepped back into the shadows and gestured for his men to move forward. "Get him boys."

"Um, Lucas," I whispered under my breath as I saw the group advancing. "They are going to fight you. They won't back down."

"You're just realizing that?" he whispered back to me.

"No, I'm just wondering what your plan is here. There's no way you can get through this."

"Listen here shrink," Lucas said with a chuckle. "We're only just getting to know one another. Don't put limitations on me just yet."

All of a sudden I felt something new rise up in Lucas. At first it was an emotional reaction, a complete state-change that overcame him entirely. His calm demeanor suddenly simmered away, and in its place a tide of complete and utter rage swept in, like a crimson red wave crashing in over a serene beach.

A physical change followed very quickly. Lucas Vancino was already a big man, he was at least six feet tall and probably two hundred pounds of muscle, but as the change overcame him he grew in size. He grew to at least eight feet in height, his torso and limbs growing in size until he was a hulking mountain of muscle.

"What the fuck?!" I gasped.

Vancino simply smiled back at me, his voice deeper now from the change. "Old family trait," he said. "Hold on darling."

A couple of the vampires ahead of us were taken aback as they saw the rapid change come over Lucas. It seemed they were afraid of his reputation, and perhaps hadn't seen the full gamut of his abilities. *Perhaps Lucas really could do this?*

My human eyes struggled to keep up as the fight exploded into action all around us. I saw the blur of a few vampires and then we were moving just as quickly. For the next few seconds the world was a confusing tangle of light and shadow, Lucas holding me in one arm as he rocketed around the room with superhuman speed.

Every couple of seconds I heard the scream of another man, followed by the crunch of a fist or the sound of an attacking blow whistling over our heads. It was over almost as quickly as it began, and when Lucas came to a stop he was back in his original starting position, his chest only slightly rising and falling from the short window of chaos.

I was dizzy but got myself together quickly to see the aftermath of the confusing fight. In front of us a dozen vampires from the group rolled around on the floor, wailing in agony as they clutched broken limbs and body parts. Beyond them was the leader, standing silent in terror, and the men remaining behind him that hadn't yet joined the fight.

"So," Lucas said. "What do you say? Are you going to let me through or not?"

The leader opened and closed his mouth, too scared to get the words out. He finally managed, stammering the syllables as he tripped over his own tongue. "Go, o-o-of course!"

"That's what I thought," Lucas said through a dark grin. He advanced forward through the tunnel, stepping over the writhing masses he had left in his wake. The group ahead of us parted like an ocean, not one of them daring to take their eyes off Lucas.

"Just what the hell are you?" I said to the vampire as he carried me further into the underground tunnel, dark and unknown to me. I watched as the group blocking the way shrank into nothingness, faint silhouettes gathering themselves off the ground and trying to piece themselves back together.

"A man on a mission," he answered simply. "Nothing is going to get in the way."

I was starting to see that.

4

LUCAS

I kept tight hold of her as we made our way through the tunnels. The fight with Angelo and his little group was hardly any trouble at all, and if I was being honest it felt exhilarating to be back in the action again.

Preferably I wouldn't have to jump right in at the deep end with a fragile human slung over my shoulder, but sometimes you just have to play the hand you're dealt. Her presence didn't handicap me in anyway, I could fight a hundred Angelo vampires and barely break a sweat, but Olivia being on the frontline like that exposed her to an element of possible danger. I'm not sure why, but the idea of her getting hurt made me more furious than anything.

Within half an hour of navigating the labyrinthian underground complex, I stopped at a ladder leading up to the surface, noticing another small rabbit etched on the wall. Gonzola's instructions had been easy to follow so far, and besides the small hiccup with Angelo, there had been no other problems.

We were right under the center of Carcoza city, the heart of the central district, which was known as The Cape to the locals. Right in the middle of the city there was a humongous market that sat underneath a vast canopy of black canvas. It was actually lots of smaller sections stitched together, but it filled the entirety of a courtyard the size of three football pitches, and a three block square radius surrounding that was under cover too.

It meant there was always a section of the city where the sun could not go. As it was the early part of the morning it was the perfect place to emerge from the tunnels, and it was also close to an old safehouse of mine. For the most part The Cape was pretty dangerous, a sprawling crowd of commerce and thievery. A person could disappear here if they weren't careful.

Low-level street crime didn't concern or bother me, but I had to make sure I looked after Olivia. The vampires in this city would eat a girl like her right up. Before heading up to the surface though there was one last thing to do.

"What are you doing?" Olivia said as I put her down on the ground at the foot of the tall ladder. Looking all around I could see it was clear. The Angelo vampires hadn't bothered following us, and if the prison guards had come down into the tunnels yet, I couldn't hear any sign of them. It was possible they had found Gonzola's entrance point now, but even if they were coming this way I still had a thirty minute lead on them.

I walked up to a fuse box on the wall near the ladder and tried the door. It was locked. Prying my fingers around the metal lip I peeled back the door and ripped the box open.

"Christ, you must be as strong as a gorilla," Olivia said while she observed me. "Are you going to tell me what you're doing?"

Inside the fuse box there was a small package that Gonzola had stored for me. I pulled it out, crouched down and opened it up, pulling out the street clothes he had stashed here. There were a few more packs in the fuse box for other inmates that were due to come this way, but it looked like we were the first to claim one.

"Getting changed," I said and started to undress, not hesitating as I stripped out of my prison clothes and threw them onto the ground with little care. Olivia suddenly decided she was bashful and covered her eyes while turning around.

"Give me a warning, Christ! That's more than I needed to see at this time in the morning."

I couldn't help but laugh as I pulled on some socks and underwear. "What's the matter, cupcake? Never seen a cock before?"

"It's not—" she started, tripping over her own words as she tried to hide her embarrassment. The feisty little brunette still had her back to me, holding her hands over her eyes in a prudish way, like a horse in blinkers. If I didn't know any better, she wasn't embarrassed about me stripping off in front of her, she was embarrassed about how that made her feel.

I slipped the rest of the ensemble on. Dark cargo trousers, a black shirt, heavy black boots and a belt thick enough to hang a rhino. All the while I focused my senses on the furious little brunette, smiling to myself as I deciphered her physical reaction.

Elevated heartbeat. Trace of perspiration on her skin. Slight pheromonal change in response to me undressing.

If I didn't know any better, I'd say she was horny as fuck.

"You can turn around now," I ordered. She gave me a testing glance and dropped her hands upon seeing me clothed.

"A heads up next time would be nice," she said. "What about me? Don't I get a change of clothes?"

"You're already in civilian garb. You don't need a change of clothes."

"So what now then? We head up to the surface?"

"Pretty much." I looked up at the ladder on the wall. By the looks of things we were about five hundred feet below the surface. "This brings us up in the center, in an area known as The Cape. It's the central few blocks of Carcoza, and it's always under permanent shade."

"Great. How far to the station? Can you get me there?"

"Station?" I said with an amused and questioning smile.

"Yes, I'm getting out of this godforsaken city. I appreciate you getting me out of the dicey situation back there. I have to say you've been more than honorable considering your reputation. I'll make sure my observations make it back to the board. I do believe you're inno-cent, despite the accusations held against you."

"Well, aren't you just a basket full of cupcakes and roses."

She wrinkled her nose and looked offended. "What's that supposed to mean?"

"If you haven't been paying attention my captors are not rational men. I faked my death to get out of that prison. As far as they're concerned, I'm dead. Your opinion of my innocence doesn't mean much now, and if they catch me alive, I guarantee the first thing they'll do is to kill me."

"What about the other vampires that have seen you get out alive? That group back in the tunnel?"

"Inmates don't snitch on other inmates, no matter how much they hate one another. It's the one code we have in Carcoza prison, and everyone adheres to it. Breaking that code is a guaranteed death sentence from your other inmates, even if they are your closest brother."

"Okay, whatever. Just get me to the station. I'll get out of this city and you can disappear into the shadows, or whatever it is you plan to do." I couldn't help smiling at her self-assurance. "What's so funny? Why do you keep looking at me like that?"

"Because you're awfully dumb for someone so smart. Maybe it's lucky you're so pretty. Makes up for the moments when your brain ain't putting together the full picture."

"Is that so. Well why don't you just go ahead and tell me what I am missing here?" she said, folding her arms as she did so.

I took a step forward, closing the distance between myself and the bratty brunette. "Number one, you're working for the prison, so I can hardly trust you to go out there on your own."

"You don't have to worry about—"

"Number two," I said, placing a finger against her lips to shush her. "You're not going to survive for three seconds out there alone in the city. I don't know if you noticed, but every vampire from here to Carcoza waste would ravage you at the drop of a hat."

"I beg your pardon!—"

This time I clamped my hand over her mouth. "Number three, I think we're only just getting started with one another darling. I've been inside on my own for a very long time, and a beautiful woman just fell right into my lap. You think I'm about to let you slip through my fingers just like that?" I curled a strand of her deep brown hair around one of my fingers. A dark chuckle erupted from my chest. "Very unlikely."

She tore my hand away and took a step back. "You stay the fuck away from me! You don't get to talk to me like this!"

"And what are you going to do about it?" I said with an amused growl.

She swung for me without answering, a small section of iron rebar held firmly in her hand as a deadly baton. I had no idea where she had gotten it, or where she'd been hiding it, but I had to give it to the bratty little shrink, she was certainly resourceful when she wanted to be.

The doctor brought her arm down in a straight arc, aiming the rebar directly for my head. A normal man would most likely have been taken off guard, but my vampire senses had no problem detecting the attack at all. I practically watched her move in slow motion, waiting until the very last second before I responded with my lightning fast speed.

In one swift move I grabbed her arm by the wrist, twisted it around until it was pinned behind her back and slammed her up against the wall. The rebar rattled to the ground and then it came to a stop, the feisty little brunette squealing out in pain as I crushed my weight against her.

"Get off me!" she barked. "Let me go!" She squirmed against me, that delicious little bubble butt of hers grinding against my crotch. My cock went hard in an instant, a long iron rod pressing up against her crack, digging in as I applied pressure with my weight. She fell silent immediately, and her cheeks turned a brilliant crimson red.

"What is that?!" she gasped.

Inches separated our faces, my mouth right next to her ear. I could hear her breathing, fast, short, nervous. "What's the matter little girly?" I growled. "Are you starting to realize you're enjoying this too?"

"Let me go!" she maintained. "You won't get away with this!"

I just laughed. "Oh, little girly. You have a lot to learn. Pull a stunt like that and you think you can get away scot-free? Think again."

"What are you talking about?" she hissed through her teeth.

"Why, a little lesson in respect of course," I said as I pulled her away from the wall, both her arms pinned behind her back, one of my hands easily fitting around her small wrists. "I think it's time for a little spot of punishment. Don't you?"

5

OLIVIA

*H*e pinned me against the wall, holding me firm as he kept my arms locked behind my back. For one thing I couldn't fucking take my mind of that giant erection stuck right up against my ass. I felt so god damned hot it was almost impossible to focus on how much I wanted to hate this guy right now.

"I think it's time for a little spot of punishment. Don't you?" he growled into my ear, his voice rife with amusement and dark delight. Glimpsing his emotional state it was clear to me there was only one thing on his mind. He was horny, and his body beat with the fury of a wild and fiery desire.

An image came into my head without warning, vivid and graphic, I saw the giant muscular vampire naked, his eyes all black, his perfect body covered in a sheen of sweat. Locked in a dark room with him, the brute throwing me onto a bed and stripping my clothes away as he did whatever he wanted with me.

Jesus Christ Olivia, get it together! I told myself as I tried to push the invasive thoughts away.

One thing was for sure, I was more messed up in the head than I realized. My nipples were hard as diamonds and I could feel a warm pool of damp on my panties, all from being thrown around and pinned against a wall like I was nothing.

Was I really this much of a degenerate?

I shook my head and tried to keep my thoughts focused. I knew that it was a common reaction to feel a sexual response when engaged in physical altercations. Plenty of men and women had healthy sexual fantasies about rough sex, I just didn't expect to find myself turned on when set up on by some mindless and violent neanderthal.

"Let go of me," I hissed, trying my hardest to ignore the sensation of him pressed up against the back of my body. My head kept screaming out for him to rip my trousers clean off and fuck me sense-less, but I had to ignore that little primal part of my brain. *Grow up, Olivia!*

"As soon as you've learned your lesson, kitten," the vampire growled in my ear. Without warning he slung me over his shoulder once more and moved away from the ladder, prowling towards an old iron door on the wall ahead of us. With one swift kick from his leg the door blasted in on its hinges, revealing some sort of control room that looked like it hadn't been used in years. There were some terminals and two chairs. The vampire walked over to one of them, sat down and threw me over his lap.

"Hey!" I shouted in protest. "What the fuck are you doing?!"

"Teaching you a little lesson," he growled back. Although I couldn't see his face now I could practically hear the dark grin framing his taunts. What happened next took me completely surprise, with one hand still pinning my arms behind my back his other hand gripped the back of my waistband and tore my trousers down my legs, exposing my rear and underwear to the naked air.

"Stop that!" I gasped. "Just what the—"

My words cut short straightaway as his hand sliced through the air and cracked my ass. Suddenly pain and fire burst through the skin, I let out an almighty gasp and cursed his name with every expletive I could think of. He gripped my arms harder and spanked me again, his palm cracking down with great force several more times, each strike seeming to burn brighter than the last.

The first round of assault lasted maybe fifteen seconds, and during the short break that followed I found myself speechless, humiliated, confused, and downright furious. I opened my mouth again to protest and his hand suddenly lifted away from my skin, hovering in the air as if to deliver another warning strike.

I started to put the pieces together quickly and closed my mouth. He was sending me a message. *Keep arguing. The punishment will only get worse.*

"Very good little kitten," he said with dark satisfaction. "You are quick to learn I see. That bodes well for the two of us. Now let's remove the rest of the barriers separating us." The vampire suddenly grabbed the waistband at the back of my panties and yanked down, sliding the underwear down to my knees and then off my legs completely. I was now completely naked from the waist down, bent over his knee, with my naked rear in the air.

He brought his hand back to the skin and smoothed his palm over it sensuously, his firm skin brushing over me in light and possessive circles. It sent a shiver through me, a trill of pleasure that flickered from the top of my head down to the tips of my toes.

I clenched and realized I was biting my lower lip.

"Very good little kitten," the vampire growled. "You'll soon learn that obeying your master will work in your favor. Good girls get rewarded. Bad girls get punished. Is that clear?" Silence beat between us as he held his hand still on my naked rear, the air throbbing as his question was left hanging in the quiet. "Answer, girl," he demanded.

I didn't know what to say. I could tell this guy to go fuck himself, I could play along with his twisted little sexual game. I could try and get up and struggle my way out of this. All in all it seemed like silence was the most powerful option. The silent treatment. It was the only way I could win.

"Time to continue your punishment then," he said. "When I ask you a question you answer. It's only natural you want to test the new limits of our arrangement. That is fine. You will quickly see however what you can and cannot get away with."

Without warning his hand slashed back and forth, caning my ass with a multitude of firm strikes, spanking me over and over again with forceful might that was unrelenting and overwhelming. His grip tightened as he restrained my hands, pushing me down firmly as the other hand delivered its relentless discipline.

I tried to bite back all the sound I wanted to make. I didn't want to give this bastard the satisfaction of hearing me cry out, but I just couldn't do it.

Crack.

"Fuck!" I screamed, the words erupting from my throat as a shaking and trembling proclamation.

Crack.

"F-Fuck!" I yelled, the word breaking over several tortured syllables.

Crack, crack, crack.

"Fuck, fuck, fuck!"

He spanked me hard, he spanked me fast. He peppered in lots of quick strikes and then deliver hearty and firm slaps that felt as if they dug into my entire body. I had no idea how long the assault lasted, but when he finally came to another stop, I was breathless and trembling, sweat coursing over my body as he brought his hand to a gentle rest.

The tender moment of that touch sent shivers through me, my skin warm and numb from his twisted game of discipline and humiliation. I realized I was trembling from head to toe, my thighs quivering and my core clenching tight at each small movement as he delicately traced the pads of his thick fingers down the backs of my thighs.

"F-fuck," I whispered, the word escaping me as he slipped his fingers down the inside of my leg and up to the wetness between my legs. I hadn't realized it so far, but I was completely slick through with lust, and as he pressed the pad of his middle and forefinger against the fold, I parted around him with ease.

A long and throaty moan rose up from within me. My body tensed and I found myself pushing back onto him, encouraging the exploring digits to sink deeper. *What the fuck am I doing?*

"Yes, little kitten," my vampire captor growled above me, pushing his hand deeper, my tightness spreading around his thick fingers.

"You're starting to realize, now aren't you? This isn't punishment at all. …You're enjoying this."

I wouldn't let myself believe that for even a second, as he curled his fingers around and found my spot a sharp shriek of delight escaped my mouth again. My entire body convulsed and shook as a wave of pleasure shattered through me. I realized then that I *was* enjoying this. My thighs only trembled like this after an orgasm, and every reaction I'd had so far suggested I—for some reason—found this entire twisted game terribly arousing.

Very slowly he pulled his fingers out, another moan escaping me as I felt him leave my body. He put them to my mouth and pushed inside. "Taste your juices slave," he ordered. "Taste how wet you are for your master."

I did.

Without hesitating I opened wide and sucked my juices clean from his fingers, the sweet and bitter wetness of my lust bursting over my tongue. Once I had sucked him clean, he brought his hand back to my rear again and spanked me a few more times.

This time I realized the cries coming from me weren't cries of pain, they were more like moans of pleasure. *God damn it Olivia, you really are twisted.*

Glimpsing his emotional state I could only focus on one real emotion now, absolute carnal arousal, and a dark well of depravity, a huge vessel of sin that held all the things he wanted to do to me.

And god, he wanted to do a lot of things to me.

"What do you want from me?" I asked, the words quivering from me as he teased my wetness with his fingertips once again.

"You need to submit to me," he said. "If you want to survive in this city, then you will have to bear my scent. Every other vampire out there has to know your mine. My slave. My territory. Mine, mine alone, and no one else."

Perhaps my arousal was clouding my thoughts, but it only turned me on more to hear him talk like that. Why would a man—or vampire should I say—like this, care so much for a girl like me? He was a criminal, yes, a dark twisted mind with thoughts that were anything but normal, but he was as alpha as a man could get, huge, muscular, handsome, a natural born leader. He could have any woman he wanted. Why the fuck would he want someone like me?

"Please," I said. "I just want—"

"You want your release," he growled. "I know what you want slave. The one thing I've been keeping from you. Pushing you to the edge and pulling back again, edging you closer and closer to the one thing you want, not giving it to you until you give me what I want. Complete submission."

"I can't—" I said. I couldn't do this. It was insane. It was crazy. I couldn't just… *submit* myself to someone. He was basically a complete stranger!

"You can, and you will," he ordered, his fingertips teasing me once again. Each delicate touch was the exact right movement, an inch of torture far worse than the last. I don't know how he was doing it, but it was like he was reading *my* mind, somehow able to know what it was I wanted, and keeping the last five percent from me.

The spanking was just to arouse me. Withholding the release I so desperately wanted. That was the punishment.

"Please," I said, straight up begging him now. "Please just let me come. Please."

I couldn't take this any longer. I couldn't understand how we'd gotten here so fast, but he had unraveled me, pushed me to the edge of depravity and pulled me back enough times that I felt as though I'd do anything he'd ask of me, just to get that sweet release.

"Apologize," he commanded. "You won't attack me again. You won't betray your master."

"I'm sorry," I panted, trying to keep focus as he brushed his thumb up and down my wet folds. "It won't happen again."

"Master," he prompted.

"Master! It won't happen again master!" *Fuck, was I really calling him that? The strangest thing was that it didn't even feel that weird. It felt kind of... right. And hot.*

"Very good" he said, and all of a sudden, he pulled his hand away from me completely and twisted us both around in a flash of movement. When it was done, I wasn't bent over his knees any more, I was crouched down on the floor before him, kneeling between his legs, my head level with his crotch.

"What?" I asked in confusion. "What's going on?" The vampire had my hair bunched up in one of his hands, holding it behind my head like a ponytail. His other hand opened those dark cargo trousers, releasing his giant and thick cock.

"You get your release when you submit fully. Until then you work for your supper. I have to mark you, so every vampire out there knows you belong to me fully. Suck slave. I need to claim you with my seed. All parts of you. If you want release then you work for it."

Holding my hair he pulled me forward and I opened my mouth, breathing out through my nose as I sank down onto his long cock. The taste of sweet and salty precum burst across the back of my throat and he held me deep against his long and thick shaft. I had no idea how big he was, but it was *big*.

"That's it, slave," he growled as he held me deep, my mouth absolutely full, his thick head pressing up against the back of my throat. After a few seconds he pulled me back right to the tip, my lips drawing long beads of saliva from his head and my mouth. I looked up at him, tears brimming in my eyes from the testing of my reflex.

Truth be told I had never been this turned on in my life. If you had told me this morning a twisted criminal would turn me into a deprived sex maniac within an hour of abducting me, I'd laugh right in your face, but it seemed that my mental resolve really wasn't half as strong as I suspected.

"Again slave. Deeper and faster. On your own this time." He kept his hand gripped on the back of my head, but loosened his grasp a little, giving me the chance to take control. That final part of my brain that wanted to argue was gone, the only thing driving me now was carnal arousal. I lowered down again, taking him in my mouth completely until the tip reached the back of my throat.

Fuck this feels good.

Without realizing it I started to bob up and down, taking his shaft in one of my hands as my mouth fell into a quick and sensual rhythm.

It crossed my mind that this was incredibly inappropriate, I had technically been assigned to this convicted criminal to get inside his mind and extract answers. Now, somehow, I was on my legs fucking his cock with my mouth.

And yeah. I was kind of loving it.

"Touch yourself," he commanded, his cock swelling in length and size as his arousal continued. I kept one hand around the base of his cock and the other moved down between my legs, the tips of my fingertips applying pressure and tracing delicate little circles over my clit.

I looked up at my vampire captor, locking eyes with him, staring at those unnatural bright pupils, burning back in my direction like two discs of fire. He smoothed his hand over my head and regained his grip, powering his hips back and forth as he started to fuck me gently.

"Yes," he growled. "That's it."

My breath started to quicken, falling in quick and shallow tides as I worked up and down his length with increased speed and fervor. All the while my other hand continued on my clit, my fingers pulsing quickly as I raced towards my own orgasm. Perhaps this vampire fucker would deny me of release, but there was nothing he could do to stop me from getting there myself, and I was so aroused now that I needed to get there.

It all began to swell inside me, a great ball of pressure at the pit of my stomach, coiling in on itself and threatening to burst through me as a wave of fire. Breath fast and rasping, I pumped my hand up and down his cock, aware that he was about to come too.

I was seconds away from coming when he pulled both my hands away and pinned them behind my back. With one hand restraining me, the other gripped my head as he fucked my mouth with his cock, he erupted, firing rope after rope of molten semen onto my tongue and down my throat, filling me with his hot and sticky seed, his cock pumping over and over again until it had nothing left to give.

He finished in my mouth, his cock pushed all the way in, my lips pressed firmly against his thick base. Once he was finally done he pulled out, strings of cum and saliva arching between his tip and my lips. I was completely out of breath and dizzy from arousal, somewhat happy that I'd managed to make him come—it tasted delicious—and also furious that he'd fucken stolen my orgasm away from me.

"You bastard," I gasped, trying to get my breath back after the intense session of pleasuring him. "You stopped me!"

He looked down at me with a dark smile, his eyes burning with rife amusement. Lightly he put one hand around my throat and moved it upwards, gesturing for me to stand. I did and he guided me forward, moving me forwards until I was straddling his naked lap. My pussy pressed up against his hard cock and I suddenly found it very hard to concentrate again.

Lucas curled his hands around my hips and rested his palms over my rear. He pulled me forward and we fell into a deep and possessive kiss.

For a few moments it was just the two of us. I wanted to pull myself onto him properly and fuck him hard, bouncing up and down until I got the release I so desperately craved. The vampire pulled out of the kiss however, one hand still gripped lightly around my throat.

"You have a lot to learn slave," he said, his eyes flickering like embers. "Do you understand?" I nodded my head absently, only really able to concentrate on the roiling desire that now consumed my every thought. He just shook his head and laughed. "You don't. Not yet. You are lost in your desire. Your head is drowning in it."

I then realized that he had pushed me to the edge so many times because he could read my thoughts. "You're reading my mind!" I gasped.

"Are you so surprised?" he said innocently. "How else will I torture you?"

"I just—"

"What, never known another that could look inside like you can? This ability is natural among my people. It's the reason I've pushed you so far. I can feel your attraction for me. Your curiosity too. It's strong, just like mine for you. The truth, slave, is that I think our meeting was not chance. I think it was fate. I think…. I think destiny has bigger plans for the two of us."

I swallowed in my throat, not sure I wanted to admit that idea out loud myself. The connection I felt with this dark stranger was unusually strong, I had to admit that, but I don't know what it meant in the grand scheme of things.

All I knew is that I needed to have an orgasm, or I was going to lose my fucking mind.

"Patience," the vampire whispered, pulling me back in for another kiss. "You will get your reward if I think you have learned your lesson. Before we go up to that surface I need to believe that you are with me one hundred percent. To say you submit is not enough. I need you to swear it."

"Swear it?" I asked.

"Swear yourself to me. Pledge yourself. Promise to give yourself to me one hundred percent. Only then will I give you what you want slave. Only then will you get what you are looking for."

I stared into those unusually red eyes, wondering if I should really commit to something like this. He was violent, dangerous, terrifying, but there was something about him I just couldn't keep myself from. And damn… how badly I wanted him.

"I swear it," I said, the words somehow feeling as though they'd been waiting to come out my mouth my entire life. "Entirely."

"No more games," he said. "No more trickery, no more doubt. You are mine now. Now questions asked. No way out."

I nodded meekly, surrendering myself to whatever conditions he put down. As I did, I felt something strange come over me, it felt like a warm shiver, a shower of sparks that trickled down from my head to my toes. "What was that?" I said, my body shivering in response. The sensation wasn't unpleasant, quite the opposite really, but it had taken me by surprise.

"Confirmation," he said cryptically. "It is done now. No going back. You're bound to me. For better or worse."

"Better or worse?"

Then with another flash of movement the vampire rushed us into a new position. Now I was on my back against the floor, my legs spread wide, the huge hulking giant of the man perched between my thighs. His bright red eyes sparkled with dark amusement and lust as he stared down at my throbbing pussy.

"It's time for your reward slave," he said, a slight smile curling on those plump lips. He lowered down and kissed me, a shower of elation erupting through my body, my hips jutting from the floor and the nails on my fingers gripping his head tightly.

Oh fuck, oh fuck, oh fuck!

I wasn't ready for this.

My body knocked and shook, every part of me contracting and tensing in pleasure as he pressed his lips firmly against me. I couldn't contain the elation that wanted to erupt through me, a high-pitched choking sound squeaked from my mouth and I threw my hand up, biting my knuckles to try and stifle my cries of pleasure.

Stomach twitching, breath racing, I squirmed below him as his lips ever so gently unraveled me.

Oh my god.

"Now, now, slave," he growled between kisses, his hot breath brushing over me as a syphon of flame and fire. "Your master wants to hear his slave's appreciation. Don't deny me of that."

With one hand remaining on the inside of my thigh, his other came up and took my hand from my mouth, pinning it against the cool concrete floor and squeezing my wrist. The floor was unwholly cool against my back, but I was so focused on the feeling between my legs now I didn't even notice it.

"Oh my god," I panted, the words squeaking from me involuntarily. My vampire captor looked up at me, his red eyes blazing with dark amusement and delight. He kissed me gently, moving with such agonizing slowness and delicacy that I thought I would go mad. "Please!" I panted. "I thought you said I could come!"

"Oh, I did," he breathed between a dark chuckle. "But I never said it was going to be fast. Or easy. Waiting for this release little kitten, I assure you, this will be a far greater torture than my hand on your rear."

He thrust his tongue inside, the firm point separating my walls, my hands both clawing out at the floor as I tried to remained tethered to this moment. He wrapped both his hands around my thighs and pulled himself in close, his tongue pulling out as he moved it up very slowly, lapping me from the base of my slit, all the way to the bud at the top.

The movement took about ten seconds, the pressure within me building all the while. My whole body started to shake, my thighs quivering so much I thought they were about to go into cramp.

He stopped at the top and flicked the bud with the tip of his tongue, drawing a very delicate circle that brought a deep and primal moan from deep within me. Most definitely he was reading my mind with each passing second. If his pressure had even been just a slight bit more I would have lost myself, exploding in the fires of a body-shattering orgasm.

But he didn't.

Every move he made was deliberate and exactly the right amount to keep me from release, pushing me further and further towards the edges of depravity, racing faster and faster to the cliff with each moment before he pulled back and left me hanging at the last second.

His hands moved up my body and he ripped open my shirt, taking my breasts in his palms and squeezing them while his mouth continued its pleasurable assault between my legs.

So many points of pleasure, so many simultaneous connections that made it almost impossible to even remember where I was, or what I was doing here.

Once again he pulled back, tongue to the very base of my slit, moving up again with an agonizingly slow move that made me whimper with every breath. Up to my bud, lips pursed, a gently suck, a flick of the tongue, moving down a little, teasing the entrance with the firm point of his tongue. He moved up and down, planting little kisses on the wet and pink skin. Even the slightest brush of his breath electrified me now.

I don't know how much longer I can do this.

"Do you think you've earned your reward, slave?" he asked, sitting back so he was on his knees. He kept his hands on the insides of my thighs, tracing his fingers delicately up and down my trembling skin.

I nodded quickly. A pathetic and desperate creature so thirsty for the approval of a man she had loathed only moments ago. "Please!" I whimpered, biting my lip as I watched him, his bright red eyes staring down with approval. From his gaze alone I could see a deep and reckoning hunger. He wanted me just as badly, but he was getting just as much pleasure from holding back and torturing me in this way, making me wait, making me whimper.

"Yes, master," I panted, stifling another moan as he let the pad of his thumb circle over my bud, tracing small circles that pushed me once again right to the edge of breaking. All of a sudden my vampire captor moved his hands down to the backs of my knees and pushed my legs back to my chest, baring me to him completely.

He moved down again and kissed my pussy deeply, his lips and tongue pushing me close to a freefall orgasm that made it feel as if the floor was being ripped out from underneath me. Without warning he moved his tongue all the way down to my other hole, his firm point circling over the tight ring of flesh, electrifying my body in a way I had never known was possible.

I was so god damned close and then he moved away again.

"No!" I cried. "No, please, no!"

His laughter was deep and strong, loud and taunting. I was starting to think he might never give me the release I so badly needed. I had lost track of time completely now, but I estimated this game of torture was getting close to twenty minutes, if not more. He had pushed me to the edge so many times that my pussy was throbbing, no shaking, with the thought of finally getting what I wanted.

He came back to me, his lips against my mouth and his hand around my throat as he claimed me in that arrogant and possessive way. I'm not sure why, but I found it so attractive, this dark and domineering alpha, teasing and playing with me like I was some giant sex toy designed for his amusement, and his amusement alone.

"How badly I want you slave," he growled between the fierce and deep kisses. "How badly I want to take my cock and thrust deep inside, fucking you until your toes curl and your nails draw lines down my back."

Yes. Yes. Fuck I wanted that too.

"Yes master, please," I begged.

He simply shook his head, those perfect lips of his curled in that damned one-sided smile. I was so wet for him I was sure I could take his giant cock with little trouble at all, even if I had doubts when I first saw its size.

"No, not yet," he maintained. "We are still quite a way from that. The human body is fragile, and I can break you very easily if I'm not careful. You've seen my true form, my true size." My mind flashed back to that glimpse of his true self, the eight-foot tall muscle monster, the all-black eyes and the primal expression. "In the deep throe of lust I will lose myself to that form, and it will take over. You have to be ready."

"I am ready."

"No, you're not. But you can be. That is what this is. Training you. Training your body. Getting you ready for the experience. You think this is torture? It is but a fraction of the test you are up against. So far you have done very well slave. Most would have passed out from frustration, or gone mad alone from withstanding so much denial."

I'm fucking close.

"But you have done well," he said, drawing a finger through my hair in a casual manner. "You have proved that you have the steel and reserve to lay with one like me. Though you are not physically ready, I think mentally you have proved yourself, and for that... you will be rewarded."

Without any further warning he moved back down my body, pinning my legs up with his hands on the backs of my thighs. He brought his tongue back to my slit and moving from the base up, lapped the entire length of me again. The pressure came back to me instantly, a whirling fireball at the pit of my stomach, threatening to break and erupt throughout me.

"Come slave," he ordered. "Come for your master."

I slapped my hands down against the floor and screamed in pleasure as the orgasm shattered through my body, exploding from my core and breaking through me as a tide of virulent fire. "Oh my god, oh my god!" I screamed, my throat hoarse and burning as the orgasm consumed me.

It was as if a great dam burst its banks, a cup overfilling with water, every part of me filled with an electrical charge that exploded back and forth, down my legs, through my arms, across my body and over my head.

My mouth rounded in silence and I slapped my hands down over and over again, my eyes screwing so tightly shut that I saw stars swimming in the darkness. Everything went quiet for a second as sound faded out, and when it came back, I heard my own high-pitched cries of pleasure, sounds choke by fast and scraping breaths.

I had no idea I could ever feel pleasure like this, but I knew one thing for certain, if this is what it meant to be by this man—this vampire's—side, then I would follow him anywhere, and do anything he said.

With time meaning nothing anymore, I clasped and gasped until the exhilarating feeling finished tearing its way through my body. Slowly but surely my breathing returned to a more normal rate, my heartbeat came back down and I felt myself relaxing into the most amazing post-orgasmic bliss. Eyes drooping a little, thoughts blurring together as I tried to focus on the present.

"My...god..." I managed. "That was...amazing."

My dark vampire captor smiled and took my hand, pulling me up into a sitting position. He gestured for me to start redressing, and I did. "We're just getting started darling, but I'm afraid we'll need to get out of here sooner or later. If I had it my way, we would have no interruptions to your training, but as things stand this isn't the perfect set of circumstances. Get dressed quickly. We go up to the surface now."

I did as he said, watching him get dressed while I also prepared for the trip up to the surface. I have to admit I was intrigued and frightened about journeying into the belly of Carcoza. I'd only seen a glimpse of the city so far and it had done more than enough to make me want to leave, being stuck right in the middle didn't exactly inspire feelings of safety or comfort.

But being next to him, Lucas, it pushed those fears back a little bit. I'd already seen how other vampires in the prison regarded him, fear in their eyes and hearts, and his showdown with that group further back in the tunnels was evidence enough that he could take care of himself.

Carcoza was definitely the last place I wanted to be, but it seemed I had the best tour guide for it, and hey, if I managed to get a few sexual thrills out of the experience then what was the harm?

"You ready?" Lucas asked as he ducked his head back around the door and into the abandoned control room. I was just pulling up my trousers and fastening my belt. I nodded and followed him out of the room. We both stopped and looked up at the tall ladder leading up to the surface.

"Is it as dangerous as they say up there? On the surface?"

"Yes." He nodded. "Though by my side you will have no problems. My friend Gonzola arranged it so a body would be left in my cell. I doubt it will fool the Manucci family long term, but hopefully it will buy us enough time to—" Suddenly Lucas looked over his shoulder and pulled me up against the wall. "Quiet! You hear that?!" he whispered.

I couldn't hear anything at first, but as I strained to listen, I heard the faint sound of footsteps in the distance. "Someone's coming," I said.

"Multiple people, running in formation. That's the prison guard. Manucci's men must have already figured out Gonzola's plan. Maybe they got to him. There's no time to run. We'll have to fight first. We can have the element of surprise though."

Without warning Lucas grabbed me and in another supersonic flash of movement we zapped across the tunnel and into a small and shadowy alcove, completely obscured from the dim light. From this position we could see the prison guards as they emerged from the shadow, a dozen of them in all by the looks of it, heavily armed and more coordinated than the unofficial gang that had hassled us earlier on.

"What can I do?" I whispered to Lucas, watching as the guard stopped by the ladder leading up to the surface, the same one we were going to use. Lucas held a finger up to his lips and we watched the guards.

"Fan out and look for them!" a lead guard shouted. "They're here somewhere! A-team, get up that ladder and search the markets, everyone else fan out and secure the area! That bastard isn't dead, and if he gets much further Manucci will see to it personally that none of us lives to the weekend!"

The group immediately split into several teams, parting and fanning out through the tunnels, a well-oiled machine of tactical espionage. Lucas and I remained crouched in the shadowy alcove, holding our breath while Lucas—I presume—put together some sort of plan in his mind.

My heart racing in my chest, I watched as a group of three soldiers started scanning in our direction. They were about fifteen seconds away, and the flashlights on their guns would find us the second they came across the alcove.

I saw Lucas glance left and right, placing a hand on the wall either side of us. The alcove was narrow enough, just wide enough to fit us both.

"How tall are you?" he whispered.

"Just under six foot, why?"

"I've got a plan," Lucas answered. "But you're not going to like it."

6

LUCAS

I grabbed Olivia and looked up at the ceiling far above us. I knew for her human eyes the tunnels would look mostly dark, but my keen vampire senses could decipher the grim shadows with ease.

As thing stood most of the guards that worked for the prison were vampires, but they were run-of-the-mill mutts, so weak in comparison that they might as well be human with red contact lenses. Few vampires had my strength, speed, or hyper-sense, so facing them in combat didn't worry me at all.

Those guns could make nasty work of Olivia though. Even though I felt invincible most of the time I had to remind myself that she was very fragile, and the idea of her getting hurt even a little bit made me... very angry.

"Hold on tight," I said, scooping her into my arms and launching up. The jump was fast and silent, and as I neared the top of the alcove, I stuck my feet out and suspended us near the ceiling, about twenty feet above the parties searching below. It was little effort to hold the position, and I hoped Olivia could do the same. "What do you think?" I said. "You reckon you could hold this?"

"Are you kidding me?!" she said in a frantic whisper. "I'm a shrink, not a gymnast!"

"All you have to do is plant your back against one wall, and your feet against the other, it hardly requires any strength at all."

"One slip up and I drop twenty feet to a concrete floor. Say hello instant death."

"Look we've not got a lot of options, you need to stay up here while I kill these guys. I can't risk you getting hurt."

"This seems like one big giant risk."

"Well I'm about to place you between the walls, so you can make a choice—"

"Wait! What's that?!" Olivia said, pointing to the wall behind me. Glancing back over my shoulder I saw a small grating set into the wall. I hadn't noticed it so far. "I could get in there, right?"

"Huh, maybe you're smarter than you look shrink. Good thinking." Keeping hold of Olivia in one arm I used my freehand to rip the grating from the wall, holding my position while she climbed off my body and into the ventilation tunnel behind. I placed the grating back into its frame. "Are you good in there?"

"Just peachy," she said. "Are you sure you can take these guys?"

I just laughed. "Olivia, you have a lot to learn about me. I'd tell you to keep your eyes open, but something tells me that won't make a difference. Stay here and stay quiet." Without another word I flipped back so I was facing the main tunnel again and looked down to study the arrangement of the search parties. There were eight vampires remaining, not including the leader who was waiting by the ladder. Two were headed over to the alcove where Olivia and I had just been hiding, and then three more groups of two had fanned out across the tunnel to cover more ground.

Holding my breath I watched quietly as the two guards moved closer to the alcove, the mounted flashlights on their guns cutting bright wedges of light in the darkness. I counted back from five in my head and stabled my thoughts around the idea of something that would infuriate me.

A new fury beat through my heart now, the idea that one of these fuckers might bring harm to my precious Olivia.

Not on my watch.

As my countdown reached one, I felt the physical change surge through me, my body growing larger and more solid, my senses sharpening even further and my strength and speed ready to explode. A small smile curled on my lips as the threat of violence lingered in the air, and I let myself drop. I fell through the air like a silent stone, an anchor of death ready to bring hurt and destruction to those that wanted to get in my way.

My feet crunched into the shoulder of one of the guards, a scream escaping him and his gun firing momentarily before he dropped to the floor under the momentum of my weight. He hit the ground and I made sure I heard his neck break before turning my attention on his associate.

All at once the guards across the tunnel reacted within a split second of my assault. In the eyes of the guards and Olivia, I knew how this scene played out: a confusing tangle of screams and desperate gunfire while a mysterious juggernaut flashed through the darkness as a silent wrecking ball of death and destruction.

Things played out very differently for me though.

First of all I jumped off the guard I had killed and turned my sights on the gun pointed at me. The other vampire was about five feet away, his gun high and ready as he squeezed the trigger. As I saw the muzzle flash I had already jumped again, gliding through the air in one swift flip, moving over his head and landing on the floor behind him. I was back-to-back with him—but he didn't know it.

I slammed my heel into the back of his knee, causing him to fall back. As he did I sidestepped and thrust my hand down into his throat crushing it in my grip and pushing down hard to burst his head against the ground.

His friend had died in three seconds. He retaliated in one. In the two seconds after that he was dead also. Now the rest of the guards were reacting.

"Over there!" one shouted. "There! He's there!"

That's when the confusing tangle of gunfire started, muzzles flashing in the distance from all directions, the tunnels alive with the sound of echoing gunfire. I slowed my breathing and felt my heartbeat fall in sync, time slowing all around me as peak-adrenaline flowed through my berserker-rage body. In the darkness my eyes deciphered the tangle of chaos, a stream of bullets hurtling blindly in my direction.

Most of them were completely wide, harmless whistles of death that would permanently embed themselves into the concrete walls encasing the tunnel. Scattershot attempts would always have a few lucky breaks though, and a wave of gunfire was going to hit me if I didn't get out of the way.

I decided my next attack would be the group closest to me, two more vampires that were about thirty feet further down the tunnel. I started running and dropped to the ground, breaking into a momentary slide to glide under a wayward stream of lucky bullets. Once they were over my head I broke out of the slide and jumped up again, skipping over another wave and twisting through the moving labyrinth of projectiles trying to kill me.

The world moved in slow motion for me, and I must admit it brought me some amusement to see their horrified expressions grow in scope as they saw the inhuman behemoth speeding towards them in the dark, a man the size of a gorilla moving at the speed of an imperceptible blur.

"Shoot him! Shoot him!" they shouted.

"I'm trying, I'm trying!" they shouted back.

Their desperation and fear was palpable, and the last thing I heard before closing the distance was the sound of their ammo clips clicking to empty.

"Boo," I whispered in a low growl, grabbing a head in each hand and crushing them together, killing both of the men instantly. Without pausing I set my sights on the next group, much easier to handle as they had run out of ammo at the exact same time. They had barely ejected their empty clips by the time I had closed the distance and advanced on them.

"Looking for me?" I said as I emerged behind one. I ripped a combat blade from a belt on his waist and slashed his throat, throwing him out of the way as I turned to face his comrade.

"No, no, please!" he begged. I didn't hesitate as I flashed forward and buried the knife in his chest, killing him instantly. My thoughts immediately went to the last remaining group, who had just finished reloading their empty weapons and were about to start firing.

Keeping my knife buried in the chest of the dead guard, I ducked behind him and crouched down, his body acting as a shield, absorbing the new wave of bullets flying in my direction.

"Kill him!" someone shouted. It sounded like the leader, who was off to my right about thirty feet. He would be the last kill. "Kill him!" he shouted frantically.

The two guards carried on with their barrage of fire, walking forward steadily as they peppered the corpse of their dead colleague. I had to admit I was in a little bit of a tight spot here; I didn't realize they were going to reload so fast. That's when I noticed a small orb strapped to the back of my shield's belt.

"Perfect," I whispered to myself and yanked the orb free from its housing. I clicked the small button on its side and listened as it let out three small beeps. Right after the third I launched the grenade forward, smiling to myself as I heard the guards scream out in realization.

"Grenade!" they shouted. "Grenade, grenade!"

It hit the ground once and exploded, erupting as a giant plasmic orb of turquoise blue fire. The sound was pretty deafening and clapped around the tunnels as echoes carried it away. Once the silence was back I noticed a slight ringing in my ears, followed by the regular silence of a conquered battlefield. The last soldier remaining, the leader, was still cowering by the ladder, his frantic breathing and terrified heartbeat audible to me even at this distance.

"Stop!" he shouted aimlessly to me in the darkness, knowing full well that his men were all dead. The ones he had sent up to the surface couldn't help him now, he was all alone. He started firing aimlessly in all directions, spinning frantically on his heels as panic set in. His fear was so great that he wouldn't hit me even at point-blank range.

With one final charge I flashed forward through the dark tunnel and apprehended the leader, my hand gripping tightly around his throat as I thrust him up against the wall. The gun clattered harmlessly from his hand, his breath shaking in terror.

"Please!" he pleaded. "Please! I'll do anything!"

"Speak," I demanded, growling the one word in a way that said *tell me everything you know, or you fucking die.*

"All I know is that Manucci got to your friend! He's dead!"

"Gonzola's dead?"

"Yes!" the guard nodded frantically. "Someone ratted him out!"

"Where is Manucci hiding?" I demanded.

"I don't know, honestly! I don't know! I'm just a grunt, they don't tell me any—!"

His words cut short as I twisted his head to the side and broke his neck. Rage beat from my chest as short and fiery breath, my pulse still racing from the thrill of violence. The words from his mouth didn't mean much, I could tell from scanning his thoughts that the guard genuinely knew nothing.

The search party was taken care of at least, but it still left the remaining problem of Manucci's secret hiding location, and how I was going to find him. I would track the fucker down one way or another, of that I was certain. Only then would my revenge be sought, and only then could I get on with my life. I was about to turn around to head back to Olivia when I heard her screaming.

"Lucas!" she shouted. "Lucas! There's something in here! It's, ahh! Get off, get—!"

Panic set in as I heard her screaming stop. I dropped the dead guard and flashed back across the tunnel, arriving at the shadowy alcove only seconds later. In one fluid move I soared up the vertical distance and arrived at the grate near the ceiling, ripping it from the ventilation shaft and discarding it over my shoulder. I heard the muffled sound of Olivia's cries from further down the ventilation shaft, accompanied by the sounds of something moving through the space.

Large claw marks were now etched onto the shaft walls, leading into the distance, in the direction of Olivia's muffled cries. I wrapped my hands around the shaft entrance and launched myself forward.

This was not good.

7

OLIVIA

$\mathcal{I}$ had no idea what happened. One moment I was minding my own business, crouched behind the grate while I tried to make heads and tails of the chaos below, the next minute I felt something grab me and pull me into the shaft.

Maybe I was too focused on trying to keep track of Lucas, but I didn't hear anything approach me, I was simply too preoccupied trying to establish if my only ticket out of here was still alive. I almost had to stifle a scream when I first watched Lucas drop out of sight, one second he was there and then he was gone, plummeting down towards the ground, surely dead.

But then I started hearing the screams. There was the rattle of gunfire, the flash of erupting muzzles and an overall sense of dread. I didn't even have to try and tune in to see what those men down there were thinking, their terror was evident enough.

Sometimes when people are in real life-threatening situations though their emotions beam through to me clear as day, like an amplified beacon, a distress signal calling out for help. In tandem I was hit with waves of feeling from Lucas in his strange berserker state, his rage clashing against the sheer terror felt by the guards.

Most of all my eyes struggled to keep up. The room was too dark for me to see much, but the screams rattling around the tunnel almost acted like a beacon, letting me know where Lucas was now. Part of me feared he was in trouble or hurt, but from the waves of emotion alone I knew he was fine.

Then there was a gigantic fucking explosion, a neon-blue ball of fire that brought about all sorts of doubts. My own fear and apprehension clouded my ability to read the situation, any of the emotions from below lost in the fog of my own adrenaline and uncertainty. With my flingers wrapped around the grating I desperately listened out for sight or sound of Lucas. It was then that I sensed another cloud of feeling altogether, something approaching me from behind, something that felt completely unhuman.

The feeling was hard to describe, there was a deep curiosity and sadness, mixed with hunger and awe. It was only when I looked back that I saw the thing behind me in the shaft, the very first thing I saw was a great opening, a wormlike mouth dripping with strings of black saliva and unending rings of sharp pointed teeth. The creature was big, so big it filled the entirety of the shaft, and it let out a screech upon seeing me.

"Scraaaagh!" it hissed. I opened my mouth to scream back, but before I could get any sound out a tendril flashed forward from the thing and wrapped around my mouth, stifling the noise before I could call for help. The next thing I knew I felt another tendril slap around my ankle and then the worm started to retreat into the shaft, dragging me with it as it pulled me into the shadows. I fought tooth and nail, trying to grab onto the smooth walls and floors of the shaft to stop myself getting dragged further, but nothing I did seemed to help.

Somehow I managed to squirm free of the tendril that was wrapped around my mouth, and then I screamed for help, shouting as loud as I could, hoping that Lucas would hear me and come running to my rescue.

"Help!" I screamed. "Help me, help!"

I was only able to shout for a second before the tendril slapped around my mouth again and permanently silenced me. The creature suddenly picked up speed, dragging me into the darkness with startling agility, terror pumping through me from the abhorrent abduction.

Desperate to be rid of the thing, I grabbed the tendrils wrapped around me and squeezed hard, trying to uncurl and rip them from my body. The creature was strong, but the tendrils alone weren't strong enough to withstand my prying hands. I ripped both of the holds from my body, kicked the worm in the area that I thought was its head and scrambled back on all fours, trying to move away from it as fast as I possibly could.

The worm screamed and hissed as I kicked it, lurching forward to try and catch me again. Now it seemed fearful of me, apprehensive in knowing that I could defend myself.

"Stay back you fucker!" I hissed, my heart hammering at a thousand miles an hour as my body went into fight or flight mode. I knew in the depths of my soul that if I gave in and let this thing take me that I would be dead in a matter of minutes. If I didn't fight back now then I *was* going to die.

I carried on scrambling back through the chute, halfway back to the grating where Lucas had originally left me. The worm continued to lurch at me, its tendrils slapping and trying to wrap around me again. I kept kicking with my feet, booting the thing as hard as I could in my desperation to stay alive.

Part of me almost felt like the pursuing creature was holding back. I half wondered why, but at the same time I didn't care. All I had to do was get to the grating, shimmy into the alcove and crawl down as fast as I could. I knew that there were potentially still armed guards down there, but I preferred my chances with them over these strange monsters.

But on the way back to the grate I saw a side chute, a branching corridor pass me by as I carried on in my retreat. It was there I saw another of the worm creatures waiting for me, its mouth open, the rings of teeth shining like a thousand tiny daggers in the low light. I opened my mouth to scream when the thing opened its throat and let out a cloud of some strange and foul fog, enveloping me at once and making the world spin all around me.

"What the—" I mumbled, suddenly feeling very intoxicated after only a few short breaths, I tried to keep scrambling backwards but it felt as though two bottles of wine had been pumped into my body in as many seconds. The last thing I felt before my strength gave up was my head hitting the metal floor of the shaft, all fight left my body and my eyes became very heavy, pulling me into a deep and dreary darkness that felt entirely hopeless.

The cold slap of tendrils wrapped around me again and the creatures started to drag me once more.

Sound was the first thing to return. I heard the wet slapping of something loud and heavy, followed by the sound of something scraping against rock, accompanied by a strange clicking sound.

A deep groan escaped me as I started to stir. I very slowly opened my eyes and saw a dim and blurry world all around me. I then realized that I was hanging upside down, my arms bound tightly behind my back. I was swinging back and forth in small circles. Blinking my eyes my vision started to come into focus and I saw that I was in a dimly lit cavern. A small fire was flickering away a couple of feet to my right. Glancing up at my feet I saw my legs were bound with some sort of disgusting black bile, wrapped tight and then suspended to the cavern ceiling far above me.

I heard the faint drip of water in the cavern, and looked around helplessly, trying to get a bearing on my situation as I wondered how the hell I would get out of this one. With no way to really control my swinging, I was helpless to turn aimlessly. After one full revolution I saw both of the large worm creatures watching me from a little rocky platform about twenty feet away from me. Both of them were about the size of a sofa, they were albino white, the many segments of their body wet and shiny looking. Neither had eyes as far as I could tell, yet somehow they seemed to be looking at me. They were both perched in an 'S' shape, moving slightly, but mostly still as they kept sentry.

A chill passed through me.

What the fuck are these things.

Whatever they were I couldn't get an emotional read on them right now, there was only a vacuous energy, like both the creatures were somehow momentarily empty. I started to realize that they weren't in charge here but must have been servants for something higher.

But what?

"I hope Ebony and Ivory weren't too rough," a refined voice said, echoing through the dim chamber. I quickly tried to throw my weight to make myself spin around so I could try and source the owner of the voice. The cavern was shaped like the inside of a giant egg. At its floor it was twenty feet across, the walls sloping up and tapering out into a wider section that formed a natural balcony. Above this the ceiling carried on and tapered back in again on itself. I was at the bottom of the cavern, dangling from the strange black string. Looking down at my feet—which was looking up at the cavern ceiling—I could see the silhouette of a mysterious figure walking in circles around a balcony about halfway up the cavern walls, just above me.

"Who are you?!" I demanded. "Where am I!?"

"You're trespassing, and in the company of wolves. Tell me. Who are you? How did you come to find this place?" the mysterious figure said calmly.

"Those things abducted me!" I said, fear giving away to anger as I tried to handle the audacity of this person. Calming my thoughts I took a few gentle breaths and tried to get an emotional read on the situation. I could talk my way out of anything. I could control anyone. I just had to stay calm and focus.

Looking up at the dim shadow I wished that I could see their eyes to establish a connection a little more easily. Still I tried my best anyway, I could get a read, things just wouldn't be clear. Who was this person, what did they want with me? What were those strange worm creatures?

The mysterious silhouette came to a stop and looked at me, silence beating between us as we stared at one another. It was almost like they were staying still on purpose, helping me to read them.

Their emotional state came flooding through all at once, charging through me as an overwhelming wave of energy that left me confused and reeling. I severed the connection immediately, panting for breath as I tried to control myself.

"What the fuck was that?!" I said out loud, swinging around wildly from my jerk reaction. I saw the figure extend a silhouetted hand and hold it in the air, straight away my swinging stopped, my body suspended in the air, a dangling pendulum somehow frozen by the distant hand of a stranger.

"That was very interesting," the figure said. They stepped forward towards the edge of the platform they were standing on, and then they kept walking, right off the edge and into the thin air, their body perfectly balanced on nothing. I watched in amazement as the figure floated down gently and touched upon the floor. Despite still being shrouded in shadow and large shapeless cloaks, something told me I was in the presence of a feminine energy.

Sure enough as they walked forward into the dim firelight, I saw the face of a young woman under the billowing cloaks. She had sleek black hair parted down the middle, pale-white skin, vividly blue eyes and a scar that ran the length of her cheek. With no doubt she was one of the most unusual looking people I had ever seen, but I couldn't ignore the strange ethereal beauty she seemed to possess.

"What happened just now?" I asked, referring to the strange energy that had swept over me after trying to read the strange woman.

"You read my emotional state," she said casually, blinking like it meant nothing at all. "I have to say I've never met a human that can do that. Manucci must be up to some really twisted shit up there, modifying humans with magic now?"

"What are you talking about?" I stammered. "Manucci?" Wasn't that the guy that Lucas was trying to hunt down? "Isn't he the guy that everyone hates?"

"Don't play dumb with me," the dark-haired woman said as she swept in close. Her blue eyes reflected the fire, seeming to blaze with a simmering ferocity that could be let loose at any moment. "I've killed plenty of his spies, and I will kill plenty more. Ebony and Ivory haven't had a proper meal in weeks. They won't hesitate to rip you into pieces, of that I can assure you."

"I don't know anything about Manucci!" I protested. "I swear! I was minding my own business when those slug things—!"

"Zetholids," the woman said sternly.

"What?!"

"Zetholids. They are not *slug things*, they are Zetholids. They are beautiful, and they are mine."

"Whatever lady, I'm just trying to tell you what happened. I was minding my own business when they abducted me. I'm not a spy!"

"Well you smell like a spy. You stink of vampire, and a powerful one at that. The only vampire I know of with an aroma like that is Manucci, the scent of an unbearable alpha."

"Look, I was working at the prison when a riot broke out. The prisoner I was interviewing abducted me and ran into these tunnels to hide. We were going to head up to the surface when a group of guards caught up to us, I was hiding in the shafts when your slug things got me!"

She considered me very carefully, her eyes never leaving mine as she listened to the information. I wished I could look into her mind again and sense what was going on, but after the first blast I wouldn't risk it again.

"You're telling the truth," she said after a long moment of reflection. Still those bright blue eyes didn't look away. It was as though they were dissecting me, unravelling my mind and pulling apart all my secrets. "And this vampire you were interviewing..." finally she looked away, her eyes focusing on some unknown spot in the distance. "He's heading this way." A small smile curled on her lips. "How interesting. Tell me, is his name Lucas?"

"You know him?!" I said.

"I know of him. How very fascinating. Perhaps the tides of change are finally moving." With a wave of her hand I saw the thick bile rope holding me upside down snap. I winced as I expected to drop to the ground, but instead I hovered in the air, my body flipping over until I was the right way up again. The woman slowly set me down, keeping one hand on me and another on an opening on the far cave wall.

"Are you a witch?" I asked, unsure how anyone could do this sort of thing.

"Quiet, I need to tame a hot-headed alpha vampire."

I was about to open my mouth again to ask what she meant, but then I saw him fly through the opening, Lucas charged into the cave as a blur of black fury, flying at the witch with his fist drawn back, ready to strike and get me out of here.

She shouted some strange and alien word, her hand outstretched and fingers flared in his direction. A shield of magical red light sprung from her palm and a deep bass note pulsed out through the cave. Lucas suddenly came to a very quick stop, frozen in midair only inches away from the witch.

"So it's true," the strange woman said with a smile, "Lucas Vancino. You finally escaped."

"Let go of me witch!" Lucas seethed, already I could see his body starting to grow as his berserker rage took hold. I could see the dark-haired woman start to tremble, as though she wouldn't be able to hold him for long.

"I will, on the condition that you calm down. I think this has all been a misunderstanding, but a fortunate one at that." the strange witch slowly let Lucas down and eased him out of her magical hold. I could tell that Lucas still wasn't sure what to think. He could easily lunge forward and kill her now if he wanted to.

"Explain yourself, quickly," he demanded.

"Relax vampire," the witch said, turning her back on him and dismissing us both with another wave of her hand. "I think we have much to talk about, you see, we both have something in common, and I think that will make us very strong allies."

"What the hell are you talking about?" Lucas said as he came over to stand next to me, an aura of fierce protection pulsing from him like a wave of heat.

"We both want Manucci dead," the woman said casually. "Now, who wants to come inside for a nice hot drink?"

With a clap of her hands the cave wall ahead of us dissolved away, revealing a doorway through to an impossibly large clearing, a hollow of moonlit trees, at the center of which was a cottage.

"What is going on here?" I mumbled in amazement.

"Magic, darling," the strange woman answered. "Now, are you coming in or what?"

8

LUCAS

The first thing I did was get close to Olivia and stay close. I couldn't believe I had let my guard down like that and potentially put her in harm's way. I didn't know who this strange witch woman was, or what the hell those two slugs things were watching us from the other side of the cave. All I knew is that the witch could have easily killed us both by now, but she hadn't.

Both Olivia and I watched in amazement as the cave wall dissolved into nothingness, leaving a large stone archway behind, one that opened up into a moonlit forest clearing, at the center of which there was a large stony cottage. I had seen a little bit of magic before in my time, but nothing like this before. Looking over at Olivia I could tell her whole world had just been turned upside down. The witch walked through the arch into the clearing, I approached Olivia and took her hand.

"Are you okay?" I asked her. "Did she hurt you?"

"I'm fine, not hurt. What about you? What happened with the guards?"

"They're all dead. I just finished with the last one when I heard you scream."

"Those things grabbed me. She thought I was a spy for Manucci."

"Huh, so maybe we really are on the same side. Have you tried to read her?"

Olivia nodded her head. "Only once, her emotional state is unlike any I have ever seen. Far too powerful for me to focus on. It almost blew me away."

We both looked back through the arch and saw the witch stop to look back at us. "Are you coming or not?" she shouted back. "It's not safe to leave this door open too long."

"Do you trust her?" I asked Olivia. She stared at the witch for a few moments before nodding her head lightly. "Yes. I think so, though I don't know why."

I felt the same, for some reason. I wasn't sure why, I just felt like it was better for us to follow the witch, instead of turning on our heels and getting the hell out of there. It was tempting just to leave and go to the surface, reclaim my old life and track down Manucci, but as things currently stood I didn't have the power to take him and his army of goons on. I needed all the help I could get, and if this was the universe sending me a sign, then perhaps it would be good to forge an allegiance with a witch.

I took Olivia's hand in mine and squeezed it. "Stay close. I think we can trust her, but we have to keep our wits about us." She nodded and we both walked forward through the stone arch in the wall, as we did I heard the air simmer. Looking back I saw the doorway dissolve once again, leaving us stranded in this strange moonlit wood.

"Where is this place?" I asked the witch.

"A little pocket dimension I crafted. I've spent some time building this place. I first made it when I was thirteen, it was no bigger than a closet. Slowly but surely, year by year, I've expanded the size of the space and now it is the size of a small town. It's mostly woodland now, my own little haven."

"This is amazing," Olivia said as she looked around at the moonlit wood. "You can access this from anywhere?"

"Mostly. It takes time to place down doorways. The rituals to build a hidden entrance like the one you just saw, it takes weeks of concentration and focused energy to set something like that up.

Doorways can't be in obvious places, I have to be very careful. I'm very protective of my little world, you should both feel privileged to come here, others haven't seen *Gardia* before. You are my first guests."

"Gardia?" I asked.

"That is my name for this little universe of mine." The witch walked up a set of stairs leading up to the wraparound porch around the cottage. It was a three-story building made of stone and crooked beams of wood. There wasn't a right angle in sight, but the curious little structure was full of charm and character. Silver moonlight glistened over a thick thatch roof, and the trees around us were tall and gnarled, giving the impression that this place was much older than it appeared.

"What's your name?" I asked as we watched the witch approach the large wooden door and draw a red symbol in the air over the surface. The latch clicked open and the door swung in. She stepped inside and we followed.

"You can call me Hazel. My real name bears too much power. Dangerous in the wrong hands, especially those of a berserker vampire. Yes, I know your secret vampire, you made it quite obvious when you tried to attack me. A berserker. How very interesting. Do you know how rare your kind is?"

"I've been told before," I said as Olivia and I walked in. The cottage was just as charming on the inside, a generously sized country home with a cozy living room and kitchen. Crooked wooden stairs led up to the higher floors.

Hazel closed the door. "Please make yourselves at home. Take a seat around the fire. I'll bring drinks over." She snapped her fingers and a fire suddenly appeared in the great stone hearth. Olivia and I exchanged another silent glance and walked over, taking a seat on a comfy looking couch.

A moment later the small dark-haired woman returned, peeling back her outer cloaks to reveal a small body. She could barely be over five feet tall, petite in every sense of the word. She took a seat across from us, a silver tray floating in a moment later with a variety of drinks and food upon it. There was blood for me, and an assortment of choices for Olivia.

"A berserker. Almost as rare as you," she said and nodded at Olivia. "It's not every day one crosses path with an empath."

"An empath?" Olivia asked with a note of confusion.

"Indeed. That is what you are," she said, pouring herself a hot cup of tea from a bright blue ceramic teapot. "Please, help yourselves to refreshments and food." We did.

"What's an empath?" Olivia also poured herself a cup of tea and grabbed some biscuits from one of the many plates now filling the table.

"A human with a special attunement to emotion, feeling, and empathy. You can see and feel emotions just like anyone else can see light and shadow. It's a very powerful gift for a human."

"What happened when I tried to read you?"

Hazel smirked. "A witch always has to be on her guard. If I allowed another witch to read me, they could take full control of my power and do whatever they wished. Your attempt to read me resulted in you finding my natural protective forces. If another witch tried that, the spell would have fought back much harder!"

"And what about those things back in the cave. The Zetholids?"

"They are trained to apprehend any trespassers that cross into my underground hideout. You have to understand that many have tried to find me. Manucci alone sends several spies. None of them return to him. He knows I hide down here somewhere, but he won't find me. Now I know that we have a common enemy you have no reason to fear my little pets. They really are quite harmless now I know we're on the same side."

"Tell us about Manucci then," I said to the witch. "What history do you have with him?"

"Much the same as you I expect. I know who you are, Lucas. I was there when Manucci set you up. I saw the dominoes fall."

My brow furrowed slightly as I relived the memories. Ten years ago the city of Carcoza had still been relatively young. It was at a split road, destined to head toward greatness or great darkness. All the city needed was good leadership, and Manucci and I were in the running to be that man.

We were both running to be the city's first mayor, and by all accounts I had the vote in the bag. At the last moment though Manucci set me up, making me out to be a mass murderer that had killed dozens of innocent women. His plan was devious, but well put together. The overwhelming evidence was insurmountable, and I was sent to prison.

Manucci was supposed to be mayor for four years after that, but since then he'd appointed himself as mayor for life, soon replacing the title of mayor for 'High Lord of Carcoza.' He was really nothing more than a gangster, but he had the whole city under his control now, and his vice grip over the entire system meant that none could overthrow him easily.

Like a true gangster he'd run things into the ground. He took the money from the poor and pushed it into the pockets of his rich friends. Now the city was a boiling pot of crime, and the only way it could be saved was by removing Manucci once and for all.

"So what's your story with him?" I asked the witch.

"He killed my sister. Another witch by the name of Zaya. Manucci imprisoned her and used her power to put his system of shit into order. He tortured her, using her magic to take control of everything. After she died, he wanted to catch me too, but I knew better. I've been on the run ever since. If Manucci gets hold of me there's no telling what he'll set his eyes on next. With more magical power his control of the city will extend across the whole country."

"Where does it stop?" I asked.

"For him? Nowhere. He wants the world."

Olivia and I looked at one another. "Well," I said to the witch, "I'm out now, and I'm going to make sure that bastard pays for what he did."

"I believe you," Hazel said, a glint of hopefulness stirring in her eyes. "Truth be told I was actually expecting a visit from the two of you."

"You were?" Olivia asked in surprise.

"Yes. Nothing specific, but I had a vision. A sign that showed me that Manucci can be toppled. I had a dream that a minotaur and a fairy came to visit me. Together they had the power to take down Manucci."

"Excuse me?" I said. "A minotaur and a fairy?"

"Symbolism in visions isn't always straightforward," Hazel said casually. "But it's very easy once you think about it. You are the berserker, the minotaur, a traditional avatar of rage and passion. And the fairy is Olivia. Empaths are rare and magical things. Fairies are gifted in the area of emotional magic, but they themselves are even rarer than empaths."

"If anyone takes Manucci down then I do it myself," I said. "It's too risky to get Olivia involved. …You are welcome to help of course, the assistance of a witch and some magic might go a long way."

"My vision dictates this campaign against Manucci can only be successful if you are aided, that includes myself *and* Olivia. You go at this alone and the same thing will happen as last time. You will lose, and this time you will die."

A heavy silence beat between us. Little as I liked it, I could feel a powerful sincerity in the witch's warning. I knew that I could take Manucci one on one in a fight, but the truth of the matter was that Manucci didn't fight fair. He had an army on his side now, and it would take everything I had to beat him.

"I can help," Olivia maintained. "My ability to read people, it's always got me what I wanted. I could help infiltrate. We could work together. We could do this thing."

I looked at Olivia in surprise. "You really want to help? What happened to getting out of this city as fast as you could?"

"Well I—"

"She knows the truth," Hazel interjected. "We are all tied into this now, our meeting was not chance, I guess you could call it a stroke of fate. Wheels have been set into motion, and there is no turning back. Fleeing now, it would mean certain death in another form. It's do or die."

"We must act quickly then," I said, keen to get this over with once and for all.

"In time, but first there are other things I must do." Hazel stood from her chair, held out a hand behind her and suddenly her cloaks flew back onto her body. "Now I know you're both in, it's time to start working."

"What do we do?" Olivia asked.

"For now you both sit here and hunker down." Hazel looked over at a curious looking grandfather clock next to the fire. "There is something I need to retrieve if we want to start our fight against Manucci. Without it we cannot win, with it, our odds are improved significantly."

"What is it?" I asked.

"A magical stone that contains trace magic from my sister's soul. I have stored it in a very secure place. I will go and retrieve it now, but it will take me some time. Maybe two to three days."

"Two to three days?!" I said in alarm. "What are we supposed to do? Just sit on our hands and wait?!"

"That's exactly what you should do," Hazel said with a smile. "Please feel free to make yourselves at home. My house is your house in my absence. Eat, rest, drink, relax. There is a guest room on the second floor. You are free to use it."

"And when you get back?" Olivia asked.

"We begin our plan to remove Manucci from power." The witch looked at me. "Lucas, I suspect you already have something in mind. Once I return with the stone, we can talk over this in more detail. And here, take this," Hazel removed a locket from around her neck and handed it to Olivia.

"What's this?"

"This is my Stratus, a magical token that represents my magical power and my oath to the powers of good. I'm giving it to you as a gesture of trust. If I go back on my word or betray another, I will be stripped of my magic completely. Hopefully this shows you can trust me. I already know I can trust you."

Hazel turned to leave, Olivia and I both stood up. "You're sure you don't need help?"

The witch smiled. "No offence vampire, but there are some things in this universe that are too terrifying even for the likes of you. I will be fine, trust me. The journey just takes time. I will be back soon. Rest, and put a plan together. Once I return, we can fight."

She started to walk across the room, heading in the direction of the front door, but within half a dozen steps she dissipated into a shower of golden sparks that faded on the air.

Olivia and I looked at one another. There was a light smile on her face, but it dropped as she looked down at my chest. "Lucas! You're bleeding! You've been shot!"

Glancing down I saw three bullet holes down my left hand side. It looked like the guards had caught me after all, and I just hadn't noticed it. I could withstand bullets to a degree, the fact that I was starting to bleed so much suggested I'd been tagged with silver.

The effect overcame me all at once, like pain after noticing a cut. Suddenly I felt my strength fall a considerable amount, I stumbled back and grabbed for something to hold onto, finding a doorframe to support me.

"We have to get them out," I winced, my words forced and shallow as I tried to keep my breathing steady. "Find a medical kit."

Olivia nodded quickly. I could see she was trying to keep herself composed, but inside she was panicking. I lowered myself down onto the ground, my head starting to throb in pain as the silver coursed through my system. Olivia ran off to find a medical kit. My eyes started to grow heavy, the cottage interior quickly growing dark.

Hold on Lucas. Hold on!

9

OLIVIA

I tried to stay calm and focused, but panic consumed me. The only thing I could think about was that Lucas was hurt and I was the only one who could help him. I ran across the ground floor of Hazel's cottage and into the kitchen, pulling open drawers and cabinets as I tried to find an elusive medical kit.

"Come on, Olivia, come on!" I shouted to myself in a chastising manner, hating that this was taking so long. I'd already been looking for several minutes now, and it felt like far too much time had passed. If Hazel had only left a few moments later she could help us right now.

How do I help him?!

As I thought the words the pendant Hazel gave to me vibrated around my neck. I looked down at it and held it in my hand. It was a pretty thing, a see-through pyramid-shaped crystal wrapped in floral strands of white silver on the end of a delicate silver chain. The stone was glowing with bright white light, and I realized the base was trying to move up and point outwards.

Holding the chain in my hand I let go of the pendant and watched in amazement as it lifted up until it was perpendicular to the floor, a narrow shaft of bright white light coming out of its base and pointing to a door on the far side of the kitchen. I heard a voice in my head, Hazel's.

In there. Nask Root.

"Nask root? Nask root?!" I said the word over and over again to myself in a blind panic, running forward across the kitchen and throwing open the door. It opened into a large pantry, its four walls lined with countless crooked shelves, upon which there were hundreds of bottles of all shapes and sizes, holding all sorts of ingredients unknown to me.

If I was trying to find the ingredient myself it would be useless, but the shaft of light coming from the bottom of the pendant carved through the darkness, stopping on a solitary square glass bottle with bright blue powder inside it. I ran forward and grabbed the bottle, breathing out a sigh of relief as I saw the words *Nask Root* written in spidery ink on cracked yellow labeling.

"What now?!" I said, running out of the pantry back in the direction of Lucas.

Water. Get him to water and apply the powder. Good luck.

With that I felt the curious connection to Hazel sever. The pendant stopped glowing and dropped back to my chest. I skidded around a corner leading back to the room and saw Lucas sat down in a doorway, with his back pressed against the frame. His eyes were closed, his head slumped to the side.

"Lucas, Lucas!" I shouted as I scrambled over to him.

"I'm fine... I'm fine..." he mumbled. "Just a little... silver... poisoning."

"Get up! On your feet! We need to get you to a bath!"

"Sure..." Lucas mumbled, barely moving as he attempted to stand up. I shoved the glass bottle into my pocket and pulled Lucas up with all my might, struggling as I threw his arm over my shoulder and headed for the stairs leading up.

Moving him would have been bad enough if he was wide awake, but right now he was almost dead weight, and he wasn't a small guy. "You smell so nice..." he slurred, almost slipping back and pulling us both down the stairs. Somehow I managed to keep him up right, just making it onto the landing in time before Lucas collapsed to his knees and hit the floor.

"Get up, get up!" I yelled, trying to pull him. It was no use, it was like an ant trying to shift a rhino.

At the end of the hallway I saw an open doorway leading into the bathroom. I left Lucas for a moment and sprinted down the hall, the glass bottle clutched tightly in my hand. I skidded across the bathroom floor tiles and hurried over to the bath, turning the taps on quickly and throwing the plug in the drain. There was an empty jug on the side of the tub, I grabbed it and filled it with cold water from the sink while the tub was still filling.

Sprinting back out of the bathroom, I ran back down the hall and found Lucas lying on his back at the top of the stairs. One hand was clutching his injured side. He was staring up at the ceiling, his eyes wide and black, muttering something quiet and incoherent under his breath.

"Time to get up!" I said, hurling the freezing cold water over him. I was surprised to see him actually sit up and gasp, crying out in agony as he clutched his side. "Sorry," I said as I helped him to his feet, throwing his arm over my shoulder once more. "But it was the only way to get you up. To the end of this hallway. Into the bath."

"Can't... much... longer..." he said, stumbling left and right as I tried to direct him forwards. We crashed against the walls of the corridor, me doing everything I could to make sure I got him to the tub.

By some small miracle we made it through the door. I clung on to Lucas with all my strength, somehow swinging him around and basically letting him fall into the bath. The backs of his legs hit the tub and he fell back, crashing into the water with such force that it sent walls of liquid spraying up over the edge.

Everything was soaked now, but I'd managed to get him to the tub and somehow got him in without hurting him. It looked like he had bashed his head a little on the way in, but I would take all the wins I could at the moment.

"Root, root, root!" I said, patting my pockets frantically as I tried to find the damned small jar. I spun around on my heels, panicking as I saw no sight of the medicine. "Where is it!"

"Floor..." Lucas muttered, his eyes barely open now. "Hall..."

I ran to the door and saw that the little glass bottle was lying on the wooden floor at the top of the stairs. I must have dropped it when I ran back for Lucas. After cursing myself loudly I sprinted down the hall, picked up the small glass bottle and bolted back to the bathroom, dropping to my knees at the edge of the tub as I threw off my blazer and rolled up my sleeves. I set the small glass bottle down for a second and gripped the hem at the top of Lucas' shirt. Pulling my hands apart I ripped the shirt open and pulled the fabric back so I could apply the powder. The water was about halfway up the tub now, I scooped my hands in and threw it over Lucas' body, trying to make sure the wounds were suitably coated.

"Arrrgh!" Lucas roared, throwing his arms wide and bracing the edge of the tub as he kicked hard. Water thrashed everywhere. Everything was chaos.

"I'm trying my best!" I shouted back, my hands shaking as I picked up the small glass bottle and emptied its contents into my palm. I had no idea what I supposed to be doing, I just put my hands on his body and tried to cover the wounds as much as I possibly could. Despite my title as a doctor, medicine was completely unknown to me, and at the moment I was acting on complete blind faith from Hazel's disembodied message.

The powder mixed with the water, forming a bright blue paste that started to froth and bubble. Lucas threw his head back and roared, his knuckles turning white from clutching the tub edge, he kicked and thrashed, water spraying everywhere as he reacted to the ointment. It was like trying to wash a crocodile while it performed a death roll.

God help me.

It only occurred to me then that maybe I should have tried to get the bullets out before putting some strange powder into an open wound. What if I hadn't really heard Hazel's voice? What if I was just hallucinating? Even if it really was her we'd only just met, *how* did we know we could trust her?

As scary as it was to watch Lucas react in this manner, my fear only amplified when he stopped all of a sudden, his cries falling into silence and his body immediately falling limp. He was unconscious, his chest still rising and falling with breath.

"Lucas! Lucas!" I said, putting my hands on his face as if that would somehow wake him. It was so quiet now in the absence of his shouting that the silence felt deafening. Only then did I notice a faint hissing sound, accompanied by a quiet and very high-pitched whistling.

Glancing down at his body I saw steam coming from his three wounds. The paste continued to froth and bubble, and from each gunshot wound I saw crumpled blocks of shiny red silver push to the surface.

The bullets!

Thinking fast I reached out and caught them in my hand, staring at them in disgust for a second before throwing them onto the floor behind me. Within seconds of the last one dropping out Lucas woke with a start, his eyes opening wide and him gasping as he sat upright in the bath.

He looked around in confusion for a moment before looking at me and calming a little. "Olivia? What happened?" Lucas looked down at his soaked clothes, his brow furrowing as he saw a torso covered in bright-blue paste and blood. The water in the tub swirled with both these colors too.

"Bullets," I said. "Silver ones. Right after Hazel left, I noticed you were bleeding. You collapsed and I had to drag your ass up here to get you out."

His eyes widened. "You got bullets out of me?"

"Well, with a little help from Hazel," I said, holding up the empty jar of Nask root.

"What's that?" Lucas asked in confusion.

"To be honest I'm not sure. I was looking for a medical kit and Hazel's voice came to me through the pendant. It helped me find this bottle and told me what to do. You don't remember anything?"

"I just remember a lot of screaming and water. I was hallucinating,

I thought I was fighting some weird sea creature." Lucas splashed water over his face and his body too. The paste crumbled away to reveal the wounds under his torso. Somehow they had completely healed, only three pale pink scars, small and circular, left as evidence that he had been hurt at all.

"How is that possible?" I gasped. "You're healed!"

"Vampires have advanced healing, but I suspect this strange medicine played a part too. Where are the bullets?" he asked.

"There," I turned around and pointed to the three crumpled lumps of silver. They were covered in the paste and blood. "I don't know what we would have done without Hazel. You were falling fast. What even happened?"

"I'm not sure," Lucas answered. "I've taken bullets before. Normal ones don't pose too much of a threat, unless they hit the heart or head. In the torso? Still hurts. I'm not sure how I could have got all the way to the cottage without noticing, unless—"

"Unless?" I asked.

"I'd heard rumors that Manucci has made all sorts of new weapons since coming into power. I do remember hearing about him tipping bullets with all sorts of different poisons."

"Gross," I said. What caused people to inflict pain like that?

"That's not even the worst of it. I heard he was tipping bullets with medical grade painkillers and blood coagulants."

"What, why?"

"I think we just saw why." Lucas nodded at the bullets on the floor behind me. "Victim gets shot. Bullet buries in their body. Pain is immediately numbed, and coagulants stop them from bleeding. Victim walks away thinking they're okay, unbeknownst to them they have silver buried inside them, a ticking timebomb just waiting to go off."

"Dear God," I said in disgust. "That's horrible."

"Yeah, and also incredibly painful. Silver does a real number on vampires. Manucci clearly isn't fucking around. Fortunately for me I had you and Hazel to help me out." Lucas slumped back in the water, looking visibly exhausted from his near brush with death. I dropped my head on the tub edge too, still kneeling on the floor with the empty glass bottle in my hand.

It had been an adrenaline filled morning, that was for sure, but at least it felt like we had a moment's rest now. In that moment's peace I realized just how grateful I was that I had managed to save Lucas, but I didn't really understand why I cared so much.

This guy was still my captor. It wasn't long ago that I cursed the ground he walked on. Look at me now, saving his life and even mourning his potential loss.

Get a hold of yourself Olivia.

"There a shower in here?" Lucas said as he pulled the plug from the tub, the water starting to drain out.

"Over there," I said, motioning to a large walk in shower on the wall behind him. Lucas look back and nodded. He winced as he pushed himself up out of the tub, his wet clothes dripping all over the place. "What are you doing?" I asked, watching as he started to strip off and make his way over to the shower.

He glanced back at me, only in his underwear now. I hated how hypnotizing his body was. "Never liked baths. I'm going to shower and get some rest. Why don't you join me?" He nodded to my body, looking down I realized my clothes were soaked through, covered in blood and paste. I hadn't even realized what a mess I was.

Before I could answer he stripped out of his underwear and stepped into the shower, a jet of steaming hot water coming down a moment later as he turned the knobs. I realized I was just sitting there staring at him, watching as the water poured down his perfect body, the clear spray running pink as it washed away the remaining blood.

"I'll just wait outside," I said. Truth told I wanted to join him, but for some reason I found myself keeping up this air of decorum. I pushed myself up to go when Lucas looked back at me, his eyes now glowing bright red with his strange vampiric magic.

"Perhaps you misunderstood, slave," he said. I saw his mouth moving, but his voice also seemed to echo throughout my mind. "Join me. We need to get clean. I've already waited long enough. I'm not going to wait longer. Undress."

That natural part of my brain was ready to fire back with sassy protest, but before my lips could even move my body started moving, peeling back my wet clothes and stripping them away until I was completely naked. I was moving to his command.

"Hey!" I said. "Stop that!"

"Silence," he commanded, snapping his fingers. Once again the sound somehow reverberated through my mind, a crack that echoed throughout my body. My feet walked forward and I pulled the glass door open, closing it behind me as I stepped under the curtain of hot water with him. He pulled me in immediately, his arms closing around my body and his lips claiming me.

I melted in his grasp, hating that he could control me like this, but hating even more just how much I wanted this.

I was in serious trouble, and the worst part was that I was enjoying it.

Help!

His hands wrapped around me, pulling me in close as I stepped under the hot water. He pulled me in tight, his lips opening against mine, his soft lips claiming me, his tongue slipping into my mouth and moving around.

I hummed with pleasure, closing my eyes and melting into him completely, forgetting about everything else us around us. How could this feel so good?

"Lucas..." I gasped, moaning his name on my outward breath. His lips moved away from mine and ventured down to my neck, where he kissed and sucked the flesh, making it feel as though sparks were dancing across my skin. My head rolled back and another long and throaty moan escaped me, my wet and naked body squished up against his wall of muscle.

His cock was long and hard, pressed up against my crotch, just begging to bury itself deep inside me. There was an ache between my legs, a longing that wanted to know what it would feel like to have him there.

God I wanted him.

His lips moved further down still, his hands palming my breasts as he sucked and teased my nipples with his lips and teeth. A delighted squeal broke on my lips, my building pleasure already difficult to control. Steam rose up around us as curtains of mist, enveloping us in this private little world where there was no one else.

I let my hands trace down over his body, my fingertips exploring the various nooks and crannies of his muscled physique. His body was firm to the touch, a moving masterpiece that rivalled the most beautiful sculpture. Lucas let a hand slip down between my legs, his fingers curling into my pussy, my folds parting around his pads as he slipped inside.

"Oh God..." I moaned again, unable to control it this time. "Lucas..."

My hips bucked back and forth against him as his fingers slowly circled over my spot and bud. His sensual strokes were slow and deliberate, applied with pressure that was firm enough to make me tremble. He kissed me deep all the while, his lips held against mine while his hands unraveled my lower half.

I had to pull away from the kiss and clasp a hand around him, holding myself steady against his torso as my knees began to buck and tremble. I felt the pressure building inside of me, spinning and coiling at the pit of my stomach, a release of energy that wanted to explode and rip through me in all directions. My breathing began to grow fast and stilted.

I needed this.

"You could have let me die, slave," he said, his fingers not slowing in their torturous assault. My mouth rounded in a silent 'o', my pleasure rapidly approaching its cliff. "You could have left me here. You could have escaped."

His red eyes bore into me, perhaps expecting an answer to a question that hadn't been asked. "Yes?" I squeaked, trying to remember how to even use words as I focused on the sensation of his fingers in my pussy.

"But you didn't. You saved me." He pulled his hand away for a second, leaving me wanting. I panted desperately, dropping my head against his shoulder, the hot water still falling down all around us. "Why?"

"I… I… don't know," I said. It was the honest truth. It just felt like the right thing to do. I would save anyone if they were dying in front of me, even if they were a mass murder. Which… he wasn't. I think.

"Yes you do," he said, placing his fingers delicately on my pussy again. He pushed inside, the pads tickling my walls as he went back to the spot. "I want to hear it."

He began to stroke, flicking small circles over the sensitive area in a rhythmic fashion until my stomach started to tremble and clench. I was so fucking close. I guess I knew why I had saved him, I just didn't want to say it out loud. It felt crazy. It felt… unreal.

"Don't you already know?" I asked, panting loud as I kept my head pressed against his shoulder.

"Yes. But I want to hear it out loud."

I could practically imagine his lips curling in that slight smile, that hint, that suggestion of dark amusement.

"Because I…" I paused, willing myself to try and say it out loud. "Because I—"

"Yes?" he said, his fingers still stroking my pussy, my orgasm only seconds away.

"Because I need you master."

"Very good slave," he answered. Without another beat he grabbed my face and pulled me into kiss me, his other hand increasing its pressure as it drove me towards orgasm. I clung onto him tight, panting and moaning in delight while tides of virulent pleasure shattered through my core.

"Yes, yes, fuck, yes!" I cried, my whole body shaking as I tensed and trembled.

That really was the truth of it. I needed him. I was addicted. Yes, it had only been a small amount of time, and yes, I was fully aware that he was a twisted psychopath vampire, one that had taken me hostage, but still—I couldn't deny it any longer. I was addicted to him. I needed his touch. There was something about his presence that just intoxicated me and drew me in.

The kiss was slow, deep, and long, seconds stretching into minutes, and minutes maybe even stretching into a longer unknown. It felt like the world was spinning around us, the two of us stood atop a plinth far above anyone else. When the orgasm finally started to fade, I opened my eyes and dropped my head against his shoulder again, breathless and spent from another round of his pleasurable interrogation.

I was dizzy, giddy, diving headfirst into the pools of these warm and inviting waters.

"I think you're ready," he said.

"Ready?" I asked.

"For me to claim you. That's why you saved me. Our bond is nearly complete. Your body needs me now. It's time I took it."

Oh fuck.

I didn't really have a response, even if I did, I was sure I would just sputter and stammer my words on account of nerves. Lucas took control then—not that he wasn't in control the whole time—he shut off the shower and the water stopped falling, leaving the two of us in silence. He took my hand and we exited the shower, wrapping ourselves in large white towels that were hanging from a heated rail on the wall. My hand still in his, we walked out of the bathroom and back onto the landing, a place that had been so full of chaos only half an hour earlier.

Neither of us knew where we were going, but Lucas managed to find a bedroom easily enough. It was the door opposite to the bathroom. It was a decent sized, with a large four-poster bed set in a giant arched window that looked over the moonlit forest. The room was dim, only painted with the faint silver brush of light from the dreamy night outside. Strange shadows scattered over the walls from the trees, but the only thing I could really focus on was the bed, and the gorgeous vampire walking me forward.

We both sat down and were immediately kissing again, his soft and full lips claiming mine. The towels came off pretty much straight away, our naked bodies entwined over the soft bed covers, my pussy so wet with desire I couldn't wait much longer.

He climbed on top of me, spreading my legs wide and letting his weight press gently against me. "Tell me slave," he said as he came into kiss me. One circled gently around my throat and squeezed. "Do you want a lover, or do you want to be fucked?"

His lips traced down to my throat again, leaving a hot trail of kisses that made my skin burn with latent desire. With Lucas involved I could take either, and I was sure he could offer both sides of that coin in dazzling measure, but right now I wanted to see what the beast within him could do to me. I wanted him to let loose.

"Fuck me," I whispered into his ear, my core aching to feel the fill of his huge cock. "Fuck me hard."

His red eyes glistened with dark amusement, before giving away to a deep and shining black that gave the promise of true primal ferocity. He gripped both my wrists tight and pinned them above my head, holding them there with one hand while he grabbed his cock in the other. He pushed the tip right up against my wet slit and stared into my eyes before thrusting forward to his hilt.

"Your wish is my command."

He wasn't slow or gentle, and I didn't want him to be. With my hands pinned above my head he placed the tip of his cock against my pussy and thrust forward with one domineering and possessive stroke.

It filled me instantly, thrusting deep and hard until his base came right up against me. Once inside he held himself as deep as he could go. My mouth rounded and my eyes rolled back, my nails scratching at the bedding as I tried to keep hold of myself.

"Oh… my… god!" I gasped, my tight walls squeezing around his mammoth length and girth. It felt even better than I could have imagined.

And then he pulled back, drawing his cock out all of a sudden, pulling his hips all the way back until his tip came to rest at my opening. He was so hard and thick, the plump end of his cock nestling against my wet folds and kissing them gently in that teasing manner.

He thrust forward again, a little slower this time, inching all the way inside until he bottomed out again. I savored every little sensation, the way it felt as he slid inside of me, the hardness of him against my tight walls.

Oh my fucking god.

When he drew back again, he quickly fell into a slow and sensual rhythm, his hips digging forward, slightly pushing me up the bed from his force. With each monumental thrust I clenched around him, my thighs and stomach already trembling from the maddening lust that spiraled within me. Each time he slammed forward a shrill gasp of pleasure squeaked from my lips; my mouth unable to contain the ecstatic sounds that wanted to break free.

Lucas lowered himself onto me, his free hand seizing my throat as he kissed my mouth, throat, and breasts. Each little kiss filled my skin with lightning. My nipples were hard as diamonds.

"Mine," he growled, his rhythm and pace starting to pick up as he fucked me harder. I was moaning on every breath now, loving the feeling of him using me like this. He tightened his grip on my hands, keeping them both pinned against my head, as if he was taking away any chance I had to deny him of this moment.

For some reason that turned me on even more.

He started fucking me harder, the mattress and bed bouncing and creaking with each monumental thrust. The building pressure within me was quickly rocketing out of my control, my stomach fluttering and bubbling as an orgasm loomed imminently.

"Lucas!" I gasped, "Lucas! I'm going to come!"

The words seemed to spur him on. He placed his free-hand on the outside of my thigh and held it there, his hips slamming back and forth as he fucked me even harder. I could have sworn we had started at the bottom of the bed, but we were nearly up by the headboard now.

"Yes, yes, yes!" I said, the words cresting in volume and pitch with each passing breath. He was so long, hard, and thick. I just couldn't get over how could this felt. I never wanted it to end.

He stared down at me, his red eyes boring into me like a furnace of primal ferocity. Wild and possessive fire that had ignited my soul and forever changed me. The red shrank away to that empty darkness, those glistening shark-like eyes that were beast than man. I saw his teeth grow long and pointed and remembered just how dangerous he really was.

Pressure still building, I couldn't hold it in any longer. My hands were starting to tremble.

"Come for me, slave," he ordered. "Come for your master."

His words sent me into freefall. The orgasm exploded inside me, erupting from my core and across my body as waves of golden fire. My restrained hands scrambled to grab anything, my hips and back lifting away from the mattress while my stomach and thighs trembled in the wake of the quaking pleasure.

"Yes!" I bellowed. "Lucas! Yes, fuck, yes!"

My cries were long and loud, the orgasm lifting me out of this world completely and unravelling me from head to toe, taking me to a state that I didn't know was possible. Things only got worse when I felt him swell inside of me, his cock growing longer, harder, and thicker as he erupted too. I felt him explode, filling my pussy with his hot and molten come, his hips pumping deep and holding there until he was sure that I was absolutely full.

Whatever cries I had now were completely soundless, my high-pitched squeaking so off frequency that my moans were no longer audible. I simply wrapped my legs tight around him, my heels pinning him inside of me until I felt his cock stop pumping. I had no idea how long I was stuck at the peak of my own pleasure, I only had a faint awareness of the room around me, my world was now a blur of feeling and hasty breathlessness, the clamor of his sweaty body against mine, the scent of his musk as his lips sucked my nipples, the shiver of pleasure as he finally pulled out and dropped onto the bed beside me.

"Oh—" I panted. "My—" And again. "God—" I said, the words rasping from me in my state of blissful exhaustion. Every part of me was quivering slightly, still riding the wave of overwhelming endorphins that came from the most mind-blowing orgasm and sex of my life.

Glancing over I saw him lying there next to me, completely naked with one forearm across his forehead. His chest was rising and falling too, but he looked as cool as a cucumber otherwise. "Is it always like that for you?" I asked, still barely in control of my breath.

Lucas looked over and smiled. "No," he said with cool assurance. "It's never been that good. Ever."

I looked back at the ceiling above us and laughed, mostly because I still couldn't believe it had been *that* good. I knew that being a vampire he was stronger and faster than a regular human man, of course I knew that, but I had no idea those skills would translate into him being a god in the bedroom.

"I don't think I've ever felt this good," I said, rolling my eyes in my head as I relived the experience over and over. If one good thing had come of visiting this city, at least I'd had the best lay of my life. I noticed then that I didn't even have to reach out and read Lucas to read his emotional state, it was already there just sitting at the front of my mind, as though it was part of mine. There was the same sense of euphoria, mixed with an undercurrent of deep longing and a powerful and stirring lust.

I was feeling the exact same thing, but still found it curious how… *together* we felt. I'd never felt that with another person before. It was like I was a part of him, and he was a part of me.

Eyelids dropping, I blinked hard a couple of times to stop myself from slipping into sleep. A feeling of tiredness had come from nowhere all of a sudden, almost taking me by surprise.

"Damn," I said, "I nearly nodded off then."

"You should get some rest," Lucas said, rolling over to face me. "Being with a vampire is taxing for a human. It will feel more exhausting than normal."

"But the sex," I said. "I want a lot more of it."

He chuckled quietly. I could feel he wanted more too. Lots more. "Oh, don't you worry. You'll get it. But I can read you just as easily as you can read me. Too much too fast and you could get hurt. Let's take our time. There's no rush. I assure you, there's no shortage of satisfaction available. I'll rest with you. Just me and you. No one else."

Eyes lulling again, I felt myself smiling as I felt into a deep and comfortable sleep. I was slightly aware of Lucas shifting us both under the covers and spooning me from behind, but those sensations faded into the background as a dream came to me.

I was in a warehouse, run-down and dilapidated, looking like it had been closed for a longtime. I was on my knees with my arms tied behind my back. Looking over I saw Lucas and Hazel too, both tied and kneeling.

"The thing you need to learn is respect," a voice said ahead of me. There was a huge man in a pin-striped suit. He was bald and had to be the weight of five men. *Fats Manucci.* A man holding a pistol stood next to him. "Kill them," Fats said to the armed gunman.

I screamed as the gunman lifted his pistol and shot Hazel in the head. Next he pointed the gun at Lucas and shot him too. They both dropped to the floor, blood pouring everywhere.

"And that leaves you," Manucci said, his cold red eyes seeming to dissect my soul. "You'd probably love a bullet in the head, but I promise you, you're not getting the easy way out. I've been looking for an empath for a longtime darling. And I know you're out there."

"Let me go!" I screamed.

He just laughed and shook his head. "No. I've got you now. You're *mine.*"

10

LUCAS

After spending ten long years in a prison cell it felt amazing to sleep in a bed as a free man, especially next to a woman as beautiful as Olivia. She fell asleep sooner than I did, and for the longest time I just lay there with my arms around her, listening to the sound of her gentle breathing, feeling her body as it rose and fell with each breath.

I couldn't get over how amazing the sex had just been. Maybe it was ten years of pent up rage and frustration, but I knew for a fact that I had never connected with another person like that, and believe me, I spent many years as a young vampire running around and getting a taste of whatever I could.

It only cemented in my mind that there was something different about her, something special that just couldn't be matched by anyone else. Don't get me wrong, it was fun to tease the life out of her and treat her like my living sex doll, but there was no denying that what just happened here was special.

That tugging feeling in my chest was stronger than ever. It felt strange to me that even though I'd known this woman for less than a day I could say with absolute certainty that she was the one for me. It was well known that the bond between a vampire and their mate was strong and often came out of nowhere. I guess I always suspected I would find my mate, the human that was meant for me, but I just didn't think it would happen at a time like this.

If I had my way I would have found her right after settling my debt with Manucci. Not that I wasn't happy to have her now, but things weren't exactly safe at the moment, and as soon as that bastard found out I had a mate he would use it as leverage against me.

That's what Manucci did. He found your weaknesses—most often family members and loved ones—and used them against you. Children, the elderly, women, or vulnerable people, it didn't matter to Manucci. The thing that mattered most was the accumulation of power and wealth, and he would get those two things by any means.

He needed to go. It was time this city had a real leader, one that could drag it from the depraved depths Manucci had let it sink into.

I must have fallen asleep next to Olivia at some point. I don't know when I drifted off, and I don't even remember feeling tired. It was just so calm and quiet lying there with her in my arms that I guess sleep was an inevitability.

Being a vampire I didn't have to sleep often. One or two days a week usually were more than enough for me, but during those ten years inside I made a habit of trying to sleep more often than not. It wasn't like I was counting down to a release date, Manucci had put me away for good, but at least when I was asleep, I wasn't there. I could go anywhere else. I was free.

I don't remember if I dreamt or not, I only know that my sleep was deep and restful, probably the best bout of sleep I'd had since I'd gone into the prison. Even though I was trapped in solitary confinement for the majority of my sentence I always had a habit of sleeping with one eye open—metaphorically speaking of course, even vampires can't do that.

A lot of people inside Carcoza prison bought into the lies that Manucci carefully crafted around me. Many of my fellow inmates saw through the bullshit straightaway, but a small percent of the population, many of them happening to be vampires from the Manucci clan, had me pegged as number one on their private kill lists. A lot of inmates on the inside had them, especially if they were on the more deranged end of the mental scale.

I was no stranger to assassination attempts, and in the ten years I'd spent in Carcoza Prison I'd killed a dozen or so vampires that were hellbent on trying to kill me. Most of the time it was in the hallways when I was being transported from one place to another. Three of them in particular were in my own cell, prisoners that had stolen keys and broken in to try and kill me in my sleep.

Needless to say they had all failed.

But because of that I'd developed a habit of never really falling into a light sleep. It exhausted me in a way, but I guess after ten years of stress and constant alertness I was used to being tired and uncomfortable. Lying here with Olivia right now, falling into a perfect weightless sleep and waking up again with her still in my arms...

I might as well be in heaven.

There had been a watch in the civilian clothes kit stashed away for me. I lifted my wrist up and glanced at the clockface for the first time since arriving in the witch's strange little pocket dimension. Both the hour and minute hands were spinning around in opposite directions. It looked like time didn't mean much here.

"Great," I muttered to myself. Carefully removing Olivia from my arms I sat up and slid out of bed, the cool ambiance of the room enveloping my body. I stood up, stretched and walked over to the window, pausing to regard the moonlit forest below. My watch might not have been working, but I was pretty certain that we had been here long enough for the sun to have come up by now, if there even *was* a sun here.

Now that I thought about it there was no reason there would be a sun, or even a day and night cycle. We probably should have cleared that up with the witch before she left.

Rolling my heels silently over the floorboards, I left the room and headed downstairs, going to the kitchen to get a glass of blood. The fridge was full of blood packs, the witch had obviously stocked it well before she left. At least she'd remembered some things.

I took a pack out of the fridge and went over to the counter, grabbing a glass from one of the cupboards. My head was throbbing slightly with the hunger of bloodthirst, my temples pulsing with a relenting ache that wouldn't shift. I opened the blood pack and poured it into the glass, the red blood pouring out like a velvet waterfall, slipping neatly into the glass container like liquid silk.

My teeth grew into sharp points as I lifted the glass to my lips, my nostrils flaring as the scent wafted on the air. My eyes flushed black and I heard my heart beating in my head. I even felt a little itchy. These were all normal reactions for a vampire in the presence of blood. I lifted the glass and drunk it down, savoring the sweet taste of the life-giving nectar.

After that I downed two more packs and splashed my face with some cold water from the kitchen faucet. For a few moments I just stood there in the kitchen, watching the trees sway slightly in a gentle nighttime breeze. The only other sound in the house came from the ticking of a distant clock.

Curiosity getting the better of me I followed the sound to the strange looking grandfather clock that was in the living room by the fire. It was an odd thing, with a circular face like a regular clock, but hundreds of little hands moving around in all directions.

It looked like I wasn't going to get a clear picture of the time from this thing either. Turning on the spot I took the rest of the cottage in. It was a strange place, alien and unfamiliar to me, but there was a pleasant aura in the air, a strange golden glow that made it feel like I was at home. I don't know why I was so sure I could trust the witch, but she definitely gave off a trusting energy, and part of that energy seemed to live here in this cottage of hers.

Vampires like me weren't just faster and stronger than humans, we also had an ability to sense magical effects. The witch's cottage hummed with this quiet aura of welcoming magical energy, but underneath that I could sense the vague outline of something much grander and chaotic, a boiling pot of potential energy that builds universes and flatten cities.

It made the air feel electrical, and also made me wonder just how strong this new witch friend of ours was. Something told me she still had some cards up her sleeve, but I also remembered that she had been hiding from Manucci for a long time.

He killed her sister. Another piece of collateral for him. Another life broken for a stranger.

Maybe the witch was strong, but how strong could she be if she was hiding from Manucci? Most vampires didn't stand a chance against a decent witch. Maybe there was something I didn't understand here, I still wasn't seeing the bigger picture.

With my bloodthirst quenched I decided to head back upstairs and find my mate again. Once I was back in the bedroom I slipped under the warm covers and wrapped my arms around her. She was still asleep.

Man. I never want to walk away from this again.

Olivia started to stir, her eyes fluttered open and she stretched, looking back at me.

"Did you go somewhere?" she asked.

"Just downstairs to get a drink of blood. That's all."

"How long have I been asleep?"

"Maybe three hours. I'm not sure." I held up my wristwatch and showed her the spinning hands. "Time doesn't really seem to exist the same way here."

She turned around so she was facing me, both of us lying in close proximity to each other. I had one hand on her hip, my fingers curled around her naked behind.

"I had nightmares I think," she said hazily. "Bad ones."

I thought I had sensed a slight disturbance in her when she was sleeping. It must have been the bad dreams. "Anything you want to talk about?"

"It was Manucci. He had captured us all, me, you, Hazel. He killed both of you, and said he was going to take me prisoner. He said he needed an empath."

"Manucci?" I said, lifting a brow in intrigue. "I thought you'd never heard of him before you came here?"

"I haven't. I've never even seen a picture of him. I don't know what the guy looks like. But somehow he was in my dream still."

"What did he look like in your dream?" I asked.

"Large. Several hundred pounds, but it looked like there was fat on top of a lot of muscle. Like an out of shape quarter back. He was wearing a suit, he was bald, and one of his eyes was all white."

I shivered at the description; she had described him perfectly. "That's him all right. Which makes me wonder... how could you dream about someone you've never met before?"

"I don't know. If was... horrible," she said, a shiver passing through her. "It felt so real."

I realized then what was going on. "It wasn't a dream at all," I said. "It was a vision. A possible glimpse of the future."

I saw Olivia's jaw clench and her eyes harden. "No way. Not a chance in hell I'm letting things end that way. You really think that bastard is going to win?"

"Not if I've got anything to do with it. I'm just telling you what happened. Visions aren't concrete, they're just glimpses into potential future threads. Where were we in the vision?"

"I'm not sure." Olivia shrugged. "Some sort of rundown warehouse. I don't understand why he'd need me alive. What could he possibly need with someone like me?"

"I don't know, and I don't plan on finding out. Once the witch is back I'm going to hunt that rat bastard down and finish things once and for all. He won't have a chance to hurt you. I promise you that. No one out there will ever hurt you if I'm around. You're mine, Olivia. They can't take you away from me."

The words seemed to ease her worrying a little. She smiled, softening once more as she rested her head against my chest. "I like the sound of that for some reason," she said. I moved my hands around her waist, pulling her in close to me.

"Is that so? Is my little slave ready for another round? You know the more of my scent you carry the better."

Olivia looked up at me, her large brown eyes batting under long black lashes. It was sensual and seductive. "Oh, what are you going to do to me, master?" she said in a low and lusty voice.

I was hard in a second.

The time for words gone, I pulled her towards me, our lips crushing together in a fiery tangle of passion. I didn't have to read her mind to feel the all-consuming lust that beat through every part of her body. Nipples hard, pussy wet, body aching to feel my touch again.

That same ache burned through me. My cock was so hard it was throbbing, almost hurting to be back inside her again, filling those delicious tight walls, claiming the pussy that belonged to me.

The kiss was deep and fierce, slow and sensual, everything that we wanted to say exchanged through physical contact alone. I'd tried to hold back last time, keep back the berserker form that always loomed under the surface of my skin, wanting to break out and consume everything with its tireless rage.

This time I wasn't so sure I could keep it inside. My body started to twitch and grow, my veins growing thicker, my arms and legs getting larger with that old familiar ache. A snarl escaped my stomach. The beast wanted to be let loose. It wanted to fuck his new mate.

"Do it," she whispered urgingly, fear and curiosity evident in her voice. "I want to make love to all parts of you."

The best thing she could do was run away right now and get as far from here as she possibly could, but even I knew it was too late now. There was no escaping my real form. All of a sudden I was a spectator in my own head, lost in the lust just as much as the beast that was breaking out. I let out a cry of pain as the transformation exploded through me. Within seconds I was a good two feet taller and had an extra hundred pounds of muscle on my frame. My heartbeat through my skull like a pounding war drum, my mind racing with the driving desire of sheer primal lust.

Grab mate. Flip mate. Fuck mate.

I opened my mouth to speak, but the only words that came out were deep and guttural growls. Fuck. I really was an animal. Maybe I looked like a human, but christ, a vampire berserker was completely wild beyond appearances.

"Front," I growled, throwing her onto her stomach and forcing her underneath me. I mounted her, my legs spread either side of her as my large hands smoothed their palms over her delicious little rump. The sweet scent of her aching pussy filled my nostrils, my eyes now all black with the consuming hunger of arousal. I drew the pad of my thumb down her wet slit, growing harder as she let our a murmur of pleasure at the touch.

"Yes…" she whimpered, panting through her own breathlessness. "Fuck me, fuck me!"

I didn't need telling twice. With one hand on my dick I pushed the tip down to her glistening folds and let a deep moan shake through me as I reveled in the pleasure. It wasn't just my body that was bigger now too, my cock was longer and thicker. I only hoped she could take the size.

"Mine," I growled, thrusting forward slowly, her tight little hole spread to its absolute limits around my long shaft. She moaned on a high-pitched drawn out note, the sound lasting as I pushed my cock all the way inside her. As I bottomed out I felt her clench around me, her pussy dripping wet and trembling against my shaft.

I drew my hips back and started fucking her.

Hard.

With my hands squeezing her tight little waist I powered into her, thrusting over and over again with demented strength, driven by a listless animal furor that couldn't be tamed or commanded.

Small squeaks of pleasure erupted from her mouth with each thrust of my cock, spearing into her tight little pussy over and over, the bed slamming against the wall from the sheer speed and strength.

She clawed at the bedding, she pushed her hips up and moved her ass back, forcing me to take her deeper and harder.

"Yes!" she shouted. "Yes! Harder, faster!"

My beast didn't need encouraging. It gave up all fear of holding back and I lost myself to my animal fury, my hips slamming back and forth into my mate's delicious little pussy with unrestrained drive. Her cries of pleasure quickly filled the room, words stretching over half-breaths, squeals of delight shaking through multiple orgasms.

Her walls squeezed tight around me, clenching and twitching, trying to hold my cock deep and milk it for all the come inside. In this state now I knew I could come inside her multiple times and still keep going, and I did.

I exploded inside of her, wrapping her hair around my hand and holding it tight like a leash, one hand on her throat and the other pulling her head back. My hips powered into her, my cock fucking her hard as ropes of molten come exploded inside of her.

I kept going.

She slapped her hands against the bed over and over again, humming and crying her pleasure as I crested back to speed once more, my hungry cock devouring her little pussy and making sure that every inch of her was covered in my scent. This time I pulled out, beating my hand up and down my cock, my shaft hard as steel as I listened to her cries of pleasure.

I erupted all over her, firing strands of thick white come onto her ass and pussy, coating her with my seed and making sure that none would ever mistake her for being unclaimed. Her fingers danced over her clit, trembling and shaking as she pulled another orgasm from herself, my seed dripping down her milky pussy and running over her hand.

I had no idea how much time had passed. Maybe an hour. Maybe two. I'd lost count of how many times we'd come together, the only thing I knew is that she was mine now, our bond one hundred percent, our bodies one, with nothing to divide us at all.

Lost in the stupor of my berserker fury, I dropped to the bed beside her, breathless and spent from our marathon session together. She looked over at me, her hair matted and sweaty from the entanglement. Both of our bodies were drenched in sweat. There was nothing picture perfect about this moment, it was real passion, the chaotic heat of two lovers entwined in a furious battle of desire.

For the longest time neither of us said anything, we just lay there in our mutual bliss, lost in the aftermath of this erotic splendor. I could see her eyes drifting again, her fragile human body surely exhausted from the intense physical bout I had just subjected her to.

Slowly but surely my berserker form dissolved, my body shrinking back to a more normal size and stature, which was still bigger than most normal people. I didn't fall asleep with her this time, but I was happy to lay there in the dark next to her, listening to her breathe and enjoying the way she filled my senses.

Sure enough Olivia woke a few hours after that, rested and raring to go. We got up together, showered—fucked again while we were washing—and then we dried and dressed. We went downstairs and I made her breakfast while she prepared coffee and a drink for me. It was still nighttime outside, of course it was, it was very obvious now that there was no day-night cycle here. Perpetual night worked out better for me anyway, so I wasn't too bothered.

"It must have been a day now," Olivia said as we ate over breakfast. "Do you think the witch will be much longer?"

"I'm not sure," I began. "At least we have a safe place to stay until she—"

My words suddenly cut short as I saw a large, hooded figure float past one of the windows looking out into the moonlit wood. Olivia sensed my panic straightaway and turned around to see it too. The figure floated out of sight, looking as though it was circling the house.

"What the fuck was that?!" she whispered.

"I don't know." I stood up and motioned for her to do so too.

I had no idea what that thing was, but one thing was clear.

We weren't alone here.

11

HAZEL

Once upon a time I was mortal. I wasn't always a witch, and neither was my sister. We were only fifteen when our magical training began, both taken in by a kind old woman that saw potential in the two of us. She wanted to impart her magical wisdom upon us, and in the following years she taught us everything.

I think Zaya and I suspected we were always different, we were born in a difficult time, orphans in a genocide, two young girls navigating the fires of eastern-European genocide and total extinction.

Everyday brought the potential for death, or worse, and yet somehow my sister and I adapted, we fought, we persevered, we used our willpower to keep us safe and keep us going. Things got better when Babushka took us in. She was just a strange old woman that lived in the middle of nowhere, but Zaya and I could both feel she was different. Warmth and kindness radiated from her. I never forgot the first time we met her, running from a group of unruly Laskian soldier boys, their eyes wild with dreams of rape and murder.

Zaya and I were less than human in their eyes, two Kezerbian orphans, nothing more than rats.

It wasn't the first time we had run, we'd been doing it all our lives. This time was bad, they'd nearly cornered us, and Zaya let something slip as we fought back. Screaming no, she raised a hand and a blast of light erupted, knocking back the boys and giving us time to run.

Neither Zaya nor I understood what had happened, but we knew there was something inside of us, something we were keeping secret.

And so we ran from the village, our bare feet bloody and cold as we fled for our lives, the boys chasing close behind, keener for murder and revenge now than anything else. There was only one thing worse than being a foreigner in a genocide, that was suspicion of being a witch.

Our feet took us into the woods, where we both sure we were going to meet our fate. That was when she came from the shadows, a golden beacon of light emerging from the dark forest like an angel from above. To Zaya and I she was warmth, she was reassuring, but from the terror I saw in the eyes of those boys she was death itself.

"Thank you for escorting my daughters here safely," she said, in a voice that was somehow comforting to us and terrifying to them. "I give you two choices now, forget everything, or die."

Well one of the boys was clearly feeling braver than the others, he ran forward with his rifle ready, and with a gentle flick of her hand he erupted into a cloud of ash, instantly gone forever. The others immediately started to stumble back, only taking their eyes away when they turned to flee.

Zaya and I watched in amazement as the old woman gave another flick of her hand. The fleeing boys didn't turn to ash, but a small light left the top of their heads, none of them seeming to notice. It was only after they had left she explained it to us.

"They will have no memory of this last hour," she said. "They will go back and get stinking drunk. The body of their friend will wash up in the river. No one will come looking for you. Now. Tell me…" Her eyes sparkled with excitement. "Are you ready to become witches?"

My sister and I didn't have to think much before beginning our training. We had no idea then what was ahead of us, but becoming a witch changed me in more ways than I could anticipate. I was fifteen when I started, nearly one hundred years ago to the day. A century later now and biologically I was only ten years older. Becoming a witch slowed the aging process by a great amount, witches aging almost ten times slower than humans.

In that last century many things had changed. Babushka moved onto the next life after our training was complete, giving most of her power to the two of us. The training took the better part of three decades, three witch years. When it was done Zaya and I carried the torch of Babushka's knowledge into the world.

Now Zaya was dead, murdered at the hands of that stinking bastard Manucci, and the only way I could ever avenge her death was by helping to destroy the very bastard that had killed her.

Back when I was human moving from place to place was a case of putting one foot in front of the other. Nowadays things were different. As I left Lucas and Olivia behind in my cottage I dissolved in the air, walking across the living room and dissipating in a shower of golden sparks until I was in astral space.

It was a neutral magical void, a gateway, a system of paths that connected the infinite realms and dimensions of our existence. My mission was simple, travel to Nexus and retrieve the soul stone that held a remanent of Zaya's power. It was the only thing that could help topple Manucci.

Floating in a giant tunnel of pulsating blue light, I focused my thoughts and willed Nexus as my destination. Instantly I began to fly forward, moving at incredible speeds as I soared through the magical tunnels, navigating the infinite labyrinth with the ease of experience.

It only took a few seconds for me to arrive, my feet landing on solid ground as I materialized in the grand hallway of Nexus. It was a colossal-sized room, circular in shape, with hundreds of paths branching off from its central point. Huge columns stretched from the floor to the massive domed ceiling high above my head.

I really had no idea how big this place was, maybe half-a-mile from ground to ceiling, and probably the same just for the diameter of this hallway. I saw a smattering of souls around me, other witches and wizards going about their business, but the sheer scale of Nexus meant that it always felt empty.

"Name?" a woman said as she appeared in the air before me. She was all-red. Cloaks, skin, and hair the same shade of brilliant rouge. Only her eyes were white. She wasn't real, she was a Damigan, a magical spell designed to appear real.

"Hazel Nostrova."

The Damigan scanned me with her white eyes, confirming my identity before nodding her approval. "Welcome Hazel Nostrova. Here are the coordinates to your vault." She held out her hand, a white orb floated through the air and absorbed into my palm. Nexus wasn't a fixed thing, its layout was constantly shifting and moving every second, vault locations only staying in one place once a user arrived to access them. The white orb gave me the location of my vault.

"Warning," the Damigan said. "There are a number of dray-demons on route to your vault location. Would you like backup?"

"No," I said, feeling a little irritated of the potential disruption. "Why are there dray-demons in here?"

"We use them as pest control, they keep other things out. They are working in that sector at the moment. They will probably attack you. Just hold your ground and they will learn to stay clear."

"Great. Thanks."

Channeling my magic I floated up off the ground and began to head in the direction of my vault. Although Nexus was a magical place separate to earth, my form was very much physical here, unlike my astral form when travelling in the tunnels that connected these separate worlds.

If something hurt me here, I could die, and there was plenty of things hiding in Nexus that could hurt, or even kill, an unaware person.

In a way Nexus was like a giant bank, a place where magical users stored items of importance. An infinite number of sealed vaults held all sorts of secret treasures, and any magic user worth their weight stored items of most importance here.

Flying fast through the endless marble hallways, I kept my thoughts focused on my vault, which was a few minutes away from my entry point. The only thing in there was Zaya's soul stone, a small glass sphere that contained an echo of her magical signature. When she was alive the stone glowed with the brightness of her soul energy. Now that she was dead the stone would be dark and lifeless, but her trace signature would still be inside.

I hadn't seen the stone since I had last put it here, and back then she was alive. To be honest I wasn't looking forward to seeing the stone with its extinguished light. My stomach felt sick at the thought, a physical object that I could hold in my hand, permanently reminding me that my sister was gone, never to return.

Turning the corner I felt the location nearing in my mind, unfortunately however as I came around the corner I saw a pack of the dray-demons, humanoid creatures about the same size as myself, all grey, with no mouths and large black unblinking eyes. They moved around like apes, aimlessly scanning the endless hallways for magical intrusions.

I half-hoped I could take a longer route and avoid them altogether, but as I came to a stop the pack all turned in my direction immediately, their heads snapping to attention like a predator catching whiff of prey.

They made sound somehow—without mouths I don't know how they did it—but they did. There were at least two dozen of the things and the one at the very front let out a high-pitched *'Nnnnnng!'* some sort of cry that sounded like a metallic screech. All at once the demons started bounding in my direction, running on all fours like dogs mad with the scent of blood. I dropped to the ground and readied my magic, my hands and eyes igniting with swirls of bright purple energy.

I readied a charge of magical light in my palms and let it loose, the purple charge smashing into one of the demons as it launched at me. "Strativa!" I roared, letting the spell loose.

The magic exploded across the hallway, launching the dray-demon back into the reaches, causing a few of its allies to skitter to a skid and turn on their heels. The pack as a whole kept charging unfortunately, another launched, flying through the air with its claws stretched forward to eviscerate me.

"Blink!" I yelled, snapping both my fingers and focusing on a spot further down the hall, a couple hundred feet ahead of my current position. A second later I teleported to the location, now behind the group of dray-demons. They all crashed together on empty ground, skittering back to their feet and turning around in confusion to see I had somehow escaped their clutches.

Without thinking they charged back again. I chopped at the air, giant ropes of purple light appearing between the walls and the ceiling, tripping up the demons and knocking them to the ground one-by-one. Three managed to dodge the attacks and launched at me again. I clapped my hands together and screamed another spell, "Mitagax!"

Straight away I split into fifteen copies of myself, the three dray-demons now surrounded by a circle of my magical clones. Only one was real, the other fourteen were light reflections, but the dray-demons were stupid. They didn't know that.

Sensing they were outnumbered and out-gunned, they huddled together and gave up, cowering in the face of this magic that was strange and powerful in their eyes. I let the clones dissolve and released the magical charge coursing through my hands, returning to a more normal state of appearance.

"Permission to pass?" I said to no demon in particular. They looked at me with those strange unblinking eyes, the three of them scampering away quickly, running back to join the other fleeing demons. I watched them go with some amusement before shaking my head and continuing to the vault.

The white coordinate light in my head told me it was just ahead. I reached an empty part of the tunnel and looked up, seeing a doorway high on the wall in front of me. Floating up I landed on a balcony and saw the familiar door, one that I had not seen in many years.

"Here goes nothing," I groaned to myself, approaching the door and speaking the passcode in my mind. Straight away the large stone surface slid back, revealing the empty room behind it, occupied only by the small sack that held Zaya's soul stone. I walked forward and picked up the stone, trying to find the courage to open up the thing and see its dim surface, forever extinguished now, just like Zaya and her life.

As I went to open it though I felt a flash in my mind, another message from Olivia.

Help! Hazel! Help! Something else is here!

I could feel the urgency and panic. She and Lucas were in trouble. Something was seriously wrong. Before I ran back to help them though I had to check the stone. It felt like something was in here, but I had to be sure, I had to confirm its presence visually.

Loosening the cord I opened the bag and pulled out the soul stone. It was definitely here, but something didn't make sense. It didn't make sense at all.

I held up the stone, marveling at the dim light that still glowed within.

Zaya was still alive.

12

OLIVIA

The hairs on the back of my neck stood on end, the air somehow feeling colder as I hurried over to Lucas, who was frozen still, staring out at the windows like a dog keeping guard. He ushered me over silently and quickly, pulling me in close and turning off the lights as he pointed to the kitchen window.

"There," he whispered. "Look."

Glancing through the dark glass I saw the moonlit forest on the other side. For a few seconds there was nothing, but then I saw it, a figure passed the frame, a floating skeletal body dressed in long and flowing rags. The brief glimpse made me jump and I leaped out of fright.

I don't know why I was so scared, but I opened my mouth and went to scream 'Oh my god!' Lucas clamped his hand across my lips and stifled the sound before I could bring attention to us. "Quiet," he hissed. "Don't make a sound, whatever you do. Do you know what those things are?"

I shook my head quickly. It wasn't long ago that I thought the world was just humans and animals. This trip to Carcoza had really thrown me in at the deep end. Vampires, zetholids, witches, and now... these things, whatever the hell they were.

"They're Drowga, tortured misery spirits, enslaved under the magical hold of witches and wizards. They're like leeches, they latch onto people and suck everything out until there's nothing but a husk left. I have no idea what they're doing here, it doesn't feel like they're affiliated with Hazel."

I pulled Lucas's hand away from my mouth, making sure to speak in low and quiet whispers. "How could you know that? Hazel's the only witch around here. She said nothing else could get in this place."

"I just know. Vampires have a faint sense of magical signatures. I've already read Hazel's, and the signature moving those things is distinctly different, I mean—" Lucas paused, his brow furrowing in confusion.

"What is it?" I asked.

"Well, the signature *is* kind of similar actually, but still, it's definitely not Hazel. These things have been sent here by someone else."

"How do we get rid of them?"

"The best thing to do with Drowga is stay away or put them in direct sunlight. Seeing as this little world of Hazel's is doused in permanent night then I have no idea."

"Then let me look inside them. Maybe I can find something—"

"Olivia, no! I—"

I pushed Lucas's protests to one side and extended my focus outside of the cottage, latching onto the presence of the strange spirit. It wasn't hard to find, it was incredibly cold, a pit of misery and suffering the likes of which I'd never felt. I really didn't want to dive any deeper at all but looking inside the minds of these things might be the only way I could get them to go away.

Suddenly the world around me shrank into darkness and I found myself falling into the mind of the Drowga. Everything went cold and dark, and very rapidly I found all my sense of hope crumbling into a despair so deep and endless that I thought I might never get out of it.

Falling through a black chamber, I landed at the very bottom, arms curled around my knees, knees pressed against my chest. Looking up I saw a faint light up ahead, a small hole of light that felt impossible to reach.

There was only emptiness, bleakness, sadness. Then I saw someone approach in the darkness.

"Very interesting," the voice said. The woman stepped forward into the meager light and I saw a face that reminded me very much of Hazel. This person looked almost identical, but her hair was white. Her skin was grey and pale, her eyes black and full. "I've never known someone to voluntarily step into the mind of a Drowga before. You have balls."

"Who are you?" I asked, shivering from the cold. "Where is this?"

"The depths of the Drowga mind. My name is Zaya. I'm the one that brought them here. Looking for you."

"Me?"

"The empath. The one Manucci needs. I saw the vision, just the same as Hazel saw it. I knew somehow that she would be the one to find you. She made this place years ago, and she never closed it off to me, even after all that happened. I just had to wait for her to leave. And now… you're mine."

"You were good once," I said. "You weren't always like this."

She blinked, a solitary tear rolling down her cheek. "No. But those things are out of my control now. I simply follow orders, and my orders are simple. Get the empath. Get her mate. Bring them back. Manucci will decide the rest."

"You don't have to do this," I said, pushing my senses out and fighting the swirling tides of dread that throbbed all around me. I wanted to see inside the mind of Manucci's dark witch. I could feel something faint, the smallest beacon of light, the faintest suggestion that she was still able to be saved. "Let me look inside, I can help you, we can fight this—"

I reached a hand out to touch her, knowing that if I could make physical contact I could break through the barrier and—

"No!" she hissed, recoiling away, spinning on her heels as she threw herself. Deep forks of purple magic crackled all over her skin, her face suddenly paling, dark black veins forming under the skin. "Stay back, empath. There's nothing inside here but suffering. Don't make the same mistake as me."

"But I can help—"

"No one can help me now. Not even Hazel. I'm sorry, but my instructions are clear. Do not fight, for you will not escape. It's best you come willingly. Manucci can be lenient, if you do not waste his time."

I pulled my hand back, not willing to sacrifice myself. "I'm not going to roll over and give in. There's not a chance in hell we're going out without a fight. You must know that."

The dark witch smiled lightly. "I do. I was just hoping you might make this easy. Never mind. Let us begin."

She snapped her fingers and all of a sudden I found myself racing up through the dark chamber, through the light hole and up into the air, looking down I saw Hazel's cottage beneath me, and the moonlit woods surrounding it. Then I saw there wasn't just one Drowga surrounding the cottage, there were hundreds, all moving towards the building like water to a drain. I dropped down and snapped back into my body, coming to with a shrill cry.

I was lying on the floor in Lucas's arms. "Argh!" I screamed.

"Easy, easy!" he hissed at me, holding me still to stop me from hurting myself. "Olivia, I told you not to go in there. What happened? What did you see?"

"Zaya," I said. "Hazel's sister. She's the one that sent them here. She's the one controlling them. She's still alive, she has to be. There isn't just one Drowga, Lucas, there are hundreds. We don't stand a—"

The sound of breaking glass cut my words short. Lucas and I jumped to our feet and saw a Drowga breaking through the kitchen window. All of a sudden the sound of more breaking glass followed and as we turned on the spot we saw Drowga smashing through all the windows on the ground floor.

"Upstairs!" Lucas grabbed me and we ran up the stairs, my feet barely able to keep up with his. "Quickly!"

My brief glimpse inside the Drowga's mind was enough to know that I didn't want to feel their presence again, but even I didn't expect this sense of urgency from Lucas. We skidded onto the floor at the top of the stairs and ran up the next flight.

"Why so fast?!" I panted; my hand squeezed in his as he bolted upstairs.

"Olivia one is bad enough, but a pack like this, we haven't got a chance. They'll feed on us until we pass out and drag us back to the heels of their master. We have to run. We can't fight, we haven't got a—"

As we spilled onto the landing at the top of the next stairs more of the Drowga floated around the corner, Lucas instinctively broke into a skid to stop running into them, but it was too late, we were too close to them.

He struck out, his fist catching one of the creatures in the head. A skull shot out of its billowing robes and smashed against the wall, turning into dust straightaway. The remaining body reached out its hands and grabbed Lucas, its bony fingers gripping down tightly.

Lucas spun around, punching and kicking at more of the things, striking out wildly as he took several of them out. His hand slipped from my mine and I tried to kick one of them myself, my foot sailing through the cloaks and getting stuck in a ribcage.

"Argh!" I screamed as I lost my balance and fell back, landing on the floor with my foot still stuck, I tried to wrench it out, but it only made the ghastly skeleton thing fall on top of me. I was screaming and slapping, my hands stinging as they harmlessly met the cold bone creature within the billowing robes.

"Empathhhhhh!" it said in a voice that was a metallic whisper, sliding and slicing through the air like nails on a chalkboard. The sound cut through me and the creature's bony hands pressed down against my shoulders, keeping me pinned against the floor.

"Lucas!" I yelled. "Lucas, help!"

I didn't even know why I was shouting. A pile of the things were already on top of Lucas and I could see that he was outnumbered. He was on the floor, the Drowga on top of him with their faces only inches from him, a dark vortex of air spiraling from his head to theirs.

They're eating him. Devouring his mind and soul.

"Help! Someone, help!"

The air above my own face started to darken and twist, sucking away from me as the thing pinning me down started to feed. All at once I felt all the light inside me dim and darken, all my hope turning to ash, every ounce of warmth within me melting to the most horrible ice.

I felt my body start to go limp, my strength and resilience fading away as the creature devoured my will.

Just as I gave up hope I heard the most horrific screech, I recognized it straightaway, and I'd never heard a sound more beautiful. They broke through onto the landing, barreling up the stairs like two disgusting worms.

Ebony and Ivory. Hazel's Zetholids.

"Raaaaaaaah!" They screamed as they broke onto the landing, grabbing the Drowga in their jaws and throwing them left and right like they weighed nothing at all. They unhinged their wormlike mouths and swallowed the creatures down whole, the skeletal monsters actually pulling away and parting, almost looking as though they were retreating in fear.

The Drowga on top of me went flying as one of the zetholid bit into its foot and threw it down the hallway. I saw Lucas roll over onto all fours and tried to sit up myself as he crawled over to me, collapsing onto the ground next to shield me with his body.

Every last ounce of energy inside of me was gone, and I could only assume he felt the same, but he still dragged his ass over here to protect me.

"Nautilus!" a bold voice shouted from somewhere down the hallway. All of a sudden blinding light filled the building, so white and intense that I had to shut my eyes and cover them with my hands.

There was only light, unending whiteness all around me, mixed with a vast and empty silence.

13

LUCAS

The cottage was a wreck, demolished by the brief battle with the army of Drowga. I picked myself up off the floor and stared at the chaos around me. A jumbled carpet of bones and ragged robes made up the hallway landing, Hazel standing at the top of the stairs, her eyes and hands glowing with a radiant ultraviolet light.

Sensing that she had destroyed the last of them, she let her magic fade, her hair settling back down again as the invisible winds pouring out of her quietened down. Her eyes and hands returned to a more normal state.

I picked up Olivia and held her in my arms. She was unconscious but breathing.

"Is that all of them?" I asked her.

"I think so." She nodded. "Ebony and Ivory have gone searching the woods for any stragglers, but I think that's all of them."

"What happened here? I thought you said this place was safe."

"It is, but—well I made some assumptions, and those assumptions were wrong. I had a security flaw in this place all along. I just didn't realize it."

"Care to explain?" I asked.

"I will, but we need to get out of here first. It's no longer safe. I think it's best we go up to the surface now, though I don't have a place for us to hide up there."

"I do. We just need to get to a phone." I looked down at Olivia, who was still unconscious in my arms. "Is she going to be okay?"

"She'll be fine. The Drowga wasn't on her long enough to do any real damage. She's extra-sensitive because she's an empath, so the draining effect probably took more of a toll on her than a normal person. Follow me downstairs. I just need to grab some things and then we can go."

Hazel turned and made her way down the stairs. I followed close behind, stepping over the littered remnants of the Drowga left in her wake. I was so sure we were done for, the moment the things over-powered me I knew there was nothing that could be done, this was a serious attack, whoever orchestrated didn't want to fail.

We reached the ground floor and I followed Hazel to the kitchen, where she opened a door and went into a small pantry. She turned on a light, revealing a room lined with countless shelves containing thousands of glass bottles, all holding different looking powders or ingredients. The witch moved around the room quickly, picking up bottles and dropping them into a pocket in her robes. Her garments must have been charmed with an endless pocket or something, I had no idea where it was all going.

"Shouldn't we hurry?" I asked. "Before more Drowga come back?"

"There will be no more, I guarantee you that. It takes a long time to snare a Drowga, and even longer to snare that many. The person that sent them blew their load. This is a devastating loss for them."

"Who? Who sent them?"

Hazel scooped one last vial into her robes before turning to face me. "It was my sister, Zaya. The dark witch that Manucci has taken under his control." Hazel walked past me, heading for the front door. I followed her.

"I thought you said she was dead?"

"I… I thought she was. When I went to retrieve her soul stone I expected to find it without any light." She pulled out a small glassy stone that had a dim aura within its surface, holding it up so I could see.

"What's the light mean then?" I asked as we walked away from the cottage, heading towards the clearing where the portal been when we first got here.

Hazel slipped the stone back into her robes. "It means she's still alive. I thought she'd died at Manucci's hand, but this light indicates differently. If I had known she was still alive I wouldn't have left you and Olivia alone. Zaya was the only other person that could get into my dimension. As I thought she was dead I falsely assumed nothing could get in, but I was wrong."

"So the Drowga belonged to her. She was the one attacking us. Under control of Manucci."

"Correct." Hazel waved her hands, the thin air in front of us dissolving in a golden circle of light. The portal opened once more, leading back into the cave where Hazel had initially taken Olivia captive. "She couldn't enter the space while I was here, but once I was gone, I basically put down a welcome mat for her. I don't know how she found it, she must be scanning the Nexus tunnels for signs of my entry. It's very clever, typical Zaya really, it—"

Hazel stopped talking.

"What is it?"

"Nothing. It just… it gives me hope that a small part of her old self is still in there. Zaya was always the powerful one, her magical ability far exceeded mine, I was more resourceful though. I could do less, but I learned to do more with it to try and keep up with her. Once Manucci enslaved her, he used her mind for his ill-gotten gains. Zaya was never a dark witch, not before he captured her."

"How could a vampire control a witch like that?"

"I don't know but finding that out is part of the solution to freeing her. I expect Manucci has some sort of magical artifact that is controlling her. Until we get close to him we won't know for sure. Finding Manucci in the first place is going to be the hard part. The guy is a shadow in a black room."

"I… wouldn't be so sure," I said through a determined smile. "I'm pretty sure I can find him, and once we do, it's just a matter of killing the bastard. So. How do we get back to the tunnels from here?"

"Follow me. I'll show you."

I followed Hazel through the caves. She seemed to know this underground labyrinth like the back of her hand, guiding us through tunnels that were almost invisible to my sharpened vampire senses. A man could get lost down here if he wasn't careful, I dreaded to think what would happen if the witch wasn't guiding me.

After a few minutes the cave tunnels ended, and we found ourselves back in the underground man-made drainage tunnels that Olivia and I escaped into after breaking out of prison. The group of vampires I killed were gone now, their bodies taken somewhere into the darkness.

"I'm guessing your pets had something to do with this?" I asked as we walked past a stray boot belonging to one of the guards I had killed.

"Most likely," she said with a smile. "They have ferocious appetites; I must thank you for feeding them."

"As long as they're not feeding on me."

We stopped at the foot of the tall ladder leading up to the surface. It had taken some time, but we'd finally got back here.

"I can give us some cover when we get up there," Hazel said. "Half an hour of invisibility if you like. Will that give you enough time to make arrangements?"

"I guess we'll see," I said, putting one hand on the ladder and keeping the other on Olivia, who was now balanced over my shoulder in her unconscious state. I started climbing rung by rung, Hazel following behind me.

Carcoza city, here we come.

I'd known this city for many years. Hell, I'd been here since its beginning. Thirty years ago Carcoza was just a small valley in a dead desert, now it was one of America's most populous cities.

Stepping out from the underground sewer hatch we emerged in an alleyway about twenty feet from The Cape, the main market square at the center of Carcoza city. I breathed in the fresh air, stale and disgusting as it was, I hadn't breathed the fresh air of freedom for over a decade.

This city was repugnant and abhorrent, but in its own special way it was beautiful too.

"Why does anyone need a ladder that long!?" Hazel scolded as she finally reached the top. I helped her out and shut the sewer behind her. We'd been underground for so long now that it was almost night-time. The sky wasn't really visible from our current position because there were so many skyscrapers at the center of Carcoza, but the thin sliver I could see was the most amazing shade of crimson red.

Even with the late hour the sprawling markets were alive with the hustle and bustle of endless crowds, tens of thousands of people moving in all directions at once. A sea of brightly colored neon-signs covered every building and market stall as far as the eye could see. The tantalizing scent of street food wafted from every corner, and all around you was the constant din of vendors bartering with customers.

Before I went inside I had most of Carcoza memorized. I assumed some things had changed in those ten years, but the majority of the city would still be the same. I'd never been in this particular alleyway for instance, but I could see the Zakoshi clocktower just up ahead, the giant time piece that stood in the center of the markets. There was a line of public payphones not far from there. That was our destination.

"Follow me, and stay close," I said to Hazel. It was pretty obvious that the witch was overwhelmed by the city and its sensory overload. "Not a city girl?" I asked.

"I don't mind it sometimes," she said, hurrying her feet to stay close to me. "I just prefer the quiet most of the time."

"What brought you here then?" I asked as we approached the end of the alleyway.

"Zaya," she said, the solitary word answer enough. In the distance I saw a group of city police walking through the markets ahead, donned in their riot gear, their large pulse-rifles primed and ready to vaporize anyone going against the status quo.

I held out my arm to stop Hazel, and ducked behind a dumpster bin, pulling her with me. We hadn't activated her cover yet, and if Manucci's police saw me you could bet that things would get interesting real fast.

"How about that cover?" I prompted.

"Of course," Hazel nodded. She scooched back and sat on her knees, waving her hands through the air rhythmically while she muttered something under her breath. I stood up and peered over the dumpster. The police patrol was out of sight now, but they definitely wouldn't be far from here. In a way I couldn't believe I was actually looking at the markets with my own eyes again. It had been such a long time since I'd seen them, part of me believed I might never get to live the life of a free man.

In the distance I saw the flash of a holo-screen, one of the giant billboards that advertised endless products over the markets. The center of the city was plastered with the things, another constant source of visual stimulation to keep your eyes busy.

The screen was huge, so big that it covered the entire width of one of the skyscrapers bordering the market. My face flashed up in black and white, a giant photograph that wouldn't be missed by anyone within a mile of here. Words flashed up in bright red letters.

WANTED! ALIVE OR DEAD! ESCAPED CONVICT LUCAS VANCINO! ARMED AND DANGEROUS! PROCEED WITH CAUTION!

I rolled my eyes and turned back around to see Hazel finish her ritual. As she did a blue orb spread out from her hands and surrounded us, muting the sounds outside of the bubble a little.

"There you go," she said and stood up again. "We're basically invisible for half an hour."

"Basically?" I asked.

"No spell is perfect, though this one is close. People should move around us, and the orb will scramble surveillance footage too. All we have to do is get to your guy in the next thirty minutes."

"Easier said than done."

Just then Olivia came to. She squirmed herself into waking, I moved her into my arms and crouched, holding her while she woke up. She blinked a few times before her eyes focused on me.

"I don't think I've ever passed out this many times in one day before. This can't be good for my brain."

I laughed. "Good to see you've still got your sense of humor." I helped her up onto her feet, grateful that I had her back again. "Are you okay?"

She held one hand against her head as the rest of her woke up. "I think so. My brain is a little foggy, but I'm guessing that's normal after going up against those things. Hazel, you saved us."

"Perhaps, but it was my fault you were in danger in the first place. I should never have left. At least you had the necklace. It let me know you were in danger."

Olivia blinked and looked at the bustling markets ahead of us. "Wow. So this is Carcoza. What's the plan now?"

"I've got a guy that can help us," I said. "We just need to get to a phone. Hazel's put a cloaking spell around us. We should be invisible, so don't worry if you see any—" I paused as a group of city police came around a corner and walked right past us. I had to admit it caught me off guard a little.

"Any police?" she chuckled. "Wow, flattering image." She nodded at numerous images of me flashing all around the markets.

"Yeah, they really caught my good side. Come on. Let's go call my contact. We've only got thirty minutes of magic cover."

"Twenty-five now," Hazel pointed out.

"Well we better hustle then."

We walked through the markets as a tight-knit unit, the endless crowds seamlessly parting around the blue orb cast by Hazel. I had to admit it made it easier to get to our destination. Normally the markets were so packed you couldn't move at normal walking speed, you were trapped in this endless foot shuffle, waiting for the people ahead of you to move.

It wasn't a place for the claustrophobic.

"Well, I have to say I love this spell," I said to Hazel as we walked forward. The crowds parted around us like an ocean moving around a rock. After we walked through, they zipped back together again, not even noticing they had moved in the first place.

"I have to come up to the surface frequently for supplies, I always walk under cover. It's a dream walking through a crowded city and being completely invisible. No one bothers me."

We walked past a stall selling human slaves and all glanced at the stage. I could tell it made Hazel and Olivia uncomfortable, if I was being honest it bothered me too. I didn't have a problem with vampires and humans having private slave relationships but putting people up for sale like that and sticking a price tag around their necks, it didn't sit well with me.

The stall was essentially a small stage, and upon it there were six girls all chained to stools. The vampire running the stall was sat in a small booth at the side of the stage, one hand cradling his face while he scrolled through a holo-phone with the other. He'd given the girls leather panties, but apart from that they had nothing else on. They all looked a little different, stark hair styles and different racial backgrounds.

One of each type, try and appeal to the broadest clientele possible.

Each of the girls waved and fluttered their eyes at the crowds walking by, though most people didn't even take notice. The eyes of the slave girls were glassy and held a thousand yard stare.

"Why does no one do anything?" Olivia asked as we walked on.

"Slavery is legal here, ever since Manucci took over. There's nothing illegal about this display, as unsettling as it is."

"Why do they perform like that?" she said, glancing back to see the girls trying their best to get bought.

"They're rewarded with narcotics and punished with violence. Wouldn't you cooperate?"

Olivia clenched her jaw, clearly rattled by the blatant and ostentatious display. "When we take that bastard down and you take charge, you're going to outlaw slavery straightaway."

I laughed. "Giving orders now, kitten?"

She flashed me a lidded look and smiled. "If you want to keep calling me kitten, then yes."

We reached the clocktower and headed down the stairs that led to the subway, stopping at the long wall of public payphones. If there was one thing Carcoza had right it was its service system. With no money anyone could use a phone, get a cab, use a train and a bunch of other things. You just had to watch an advert first.

I approached the nearest phone and pressed the touchscreen, activating a three minute video advertising the services of a company that delivered girls fresh to your door. Neither of us really paid attention to it, but once it was done, I had enough credit for a one-minute phone call.

Picking up the receiver I dialed Cypher's number. He answered immediately.

"Lovely weather we're having, huh?" he said, parroting his security phrase.

"Yes," I answered. "It's just a shame about the forecast snow." That was my personalized answer, designed to let Cypher know that he was talking to a friend, and that friend was me.

"Holy shit, you son of a bitch!" he laughed down the phone. "I heard you'd got out, but I didn't really believe it!"

"Listen up, I haven't got a lot of time. I'm coming after the big guy, and I'm going to need your help. Do you have anything that might help?"

Cypher carried on laughing down the line. "Snow my dear friend, I think I have just the thing for you. Why don't you come on over and we can throw back a few cold ones and plan a revolution. Let's see, what's your position..."

"I—"

"Don't say it on the line! I've scrambled the signal so those fucks can't trace this. Ah, there. I've got you. All right. I'll send a Hermes Cab right to your position. It should be there in a minute. Hold tight and hop in when it arrives, it'll bring you right to me. Are you alone?"

"No, I have friends. Two of them."

"Well look at you making friends! I don't believe it! Hold tight and stand by. The cab will be there in a minute!"

The call ended and I set the receiver back into the cradle.

"That was a strange phone call," Hazel said.

"Cypher has been running from Manucci longer than the both of us combined. He's a crazy hacker, a brilliant bastard, but he's paranoid too." Suddenly I noticed a hovercar approaching from above, slowing its engines as it came to a stop overhead and start to lower down. Lights flashing, the crowds parted around the car as it set down on the ground. "Can't say he isn't efficient though," I said.

"Warning, landing, please vacate the area! Warning, landing, please vacate the area!" The automatic cab said until it was finally down. Hovering a foot above the ground its doors opened like wings and we all climbed inside. Once we were all in the car hovered back up into the flying lanes and took off with speed, climbing slowly in altitude until we were halfway up the height of the city's skyline, breathtaking views sprawling all around us.

"It looks beautiful from up here," Olivia said.

"It really does," Hazel parroted. "I've never seen it from this angle before."

"For all its faults this city still has the potential to be something great. Once Manucci is gone… I promise I will do everything in my power to turn things around."

"You really think you can change things?" Hazel said, looking over the cityscape.

"Hey, New York City was a dump once upon a time, right? Vegas too. Look at them both now. There are good people in these streets, we just need to stop enabling the bad ones."

"Where does this friend of yours live?" Hazel looked out the window, realizing that the Hermes cab was heading away from the city center, flying towards an area known as The Grill. "Is that… that's The Grill on the horizon!"

"The what?" Olivia asked.

"The Grill, it's the poorest part of the city, and it has the highest amount of crime too. Things are pretty crazy there. There was some infighting between political factions when Carcoza was growing up, and quite a lot of action took place there. There are blocks and blocks of buildings that were bombed out and never really repaired."

I looked out the windows of the Hermes Cab as I saw the dilapidated buildings and streets of The Grill passing below us. There wasn't much flying traffic now and I seemed to recall Hermes Cabs didn't come out here because of people attacking them from the street. This particular cab had to have been stolen and hacked by Cypher to get out here.

"What's that building over there?" Olivia said, pointing to a giant building shaped like a black glass egg on its side. The exterior of the building was covered in thousands of square panels all twisted at the same angle, making it look like dragon scales made from black glass.

"Kadivo Mall," I said. "It was the main shopping hub in Carcoza city until the troubles began. Now it's abandoned, a giant homeless camp that houses gangs and people from the street. It's pretty wild in there. A true no man's land."

"It also looks like that's our destination," Olivia pointed out, nodding as the cab started to fly down, lowering in altitude until it was flying over the sprawling glassy roof. It was heading for a flat pitch of concrete a couple hundred feet ahead, which grew in size as we approached. The cab set down and the doors hissed open. As we stepped out three women walked out of a maintenance door on the roof and trained pulse rifles on us. They were wearing stolen riot armor and their neon-colored dreads suggested none of them were affiliated with Manucci's official police force.

"State your business," the woman at the front said. She had bright red-hair, with a vibrant green undercut.

"I'm a friend of Cypher," I said, my hands held up. Olivia and Hazel did the same.

"I know you," another woman said behind her rifle sights. Her hair was bright yellow. "Lucas Vancino, the fuck that butchered all those women."

"And I already told you a million times that he was framed!" Cypher said as he came onto the rooftop. "I'm even *this* close to solving it. Lucas you'll have to forgive my wife, Varsha. She runs security around here, we don't take kindly to strangers."

"Not your wife," Varsha, the red-haired one, growled, lowering her rifle and nodding at her colleagues to do so too. Cypher ran over and we shook hands, patting each other on the back as familiar friends. I could count the number of true allies I had on one hand, and Cypher was one of them. He was tall and well-built for the amount of time he spent in front of a screen. A lot of those computer types looked the part, but Cypher wasn't a bad looking guy, he'd probably be quite successful with the ladies if he turned his computer off for a second.

"And who are the beautiful ladies?" Cypher said, turning his gaze on Olivia and Hazel.

"Olivia. Technically Lucas' prisoner," Olivia said.

"Technically my mate," I said, rolling my eyes at her joke. I waited for the witch to introduce herself, but she said nothing. "This is Hazel, a witch. She's against Manucci too. He took her sister."

"No witches allowed," Varsha said, bringing her gun back up again. Her friends did the same. Cypher looked back at his security.

"Varsha, chill, will you? They're all good. We're all on the same side here."

She shook her head. "No way. I lost friends to Manucci's witch. If this here is her sister, well I'm sorry, she's not trustworthy. There's no telling what she can do."

Without blinking Hazel raised a hand and snapped her fingers. The three pulse rifles suddenly vanished, leaving the girls with a gun-sized stick in their hands.

"What the fuck!" Varsha exclaimed.

"Pro-tip, don't bring a gun to a magic fight," Hazel said. "A puny pulse rifle isn't going to stop me. If I was working for Manucci you'd already be dead. I think it's safe to say I'm trustworthy. No?"

Varsha's brow knotted with reluctant disapproval. "I guess. I'll be watching you though."

With another snap of her fingers Hazel brought the guns back. It was a bit of a hairy start, but at least we could say everyone trusted each other now.

"So," I said to Cypher. "Are we doing this or what? How do we get to Manucci?"

A large grin spread over Cypher's face. "Tell me. Are you comfortable with the idea of kidnapping a noble?"

"Something tells me this plan is a life or death situation."

"Isn't that the mark of a good plan? Come," Cypher said, putting an arm around my shoulder and gesturing for me to follow him. "We've got work to do."

OLIVIA

This place was wild, I could feel it in the air. Sometimes I didn't have to tap into a person to gauge their emotional state or try and guess what they were thinking, sometimes just walking through a place was enough for me to get a vibe on things.

The old, abandoned mall was just that kind of place. From the moment the cab set us down on the roof I could feel a great pot of energy swirling underneath us, projecting forth the collective fears and desires of the population living within these walls. When the armed women had their guns on us, I didn't feel any fear because deep down they knew we were all on the same side.

On the surface one could judge this place as a homeless camp, a crumbling building that housed vagrants and vagabonds, people that had nowhere else to go, people that made crime their living.

I could tell there was something bigger here though, like a coiled viper waiting to jump out and strike. The beginnings of something greater.

"As you can see the old gal could do with a bit of upkeep," Cypher said as we followed him through the upper hallways of the abandoned mall. Once upon a time it looked like this place had been modern, clean, and tidy, a state-of-the-art shopping facility for rich people to spend their money.

Now… things didn't look so great. Most of the lights weren't working, and hundreds of homeless people had small living areas that lined the corridors and walkways. A person might feel uneasy with this many eyes staring back at them, but as we walked through, I felt a collective impression from the people living here.

Reverence.

Why?

"How many people live here?" Hazel asked.

"As of last count about ten thousand," Varsha answered from the rear. "But the numbers are changing all the time. People come and go. People disappear. That's the way of the streets."

"Not to blow my own trumpet, but things got better when old Cypher arrived," he said as we walked through a large archway that led into an old food court. We followed Cypher up a broken set of escalators. Once upon a time it looked like there had been a seating area set above the court, but as we came to the top of the metal stairs I saw all the tables and chairs were gone. In their place was a miniature jungle of computer terminals, screens, thousands of cables running all over the floor, and a whole bunch of technical junk that I simply didn't recognize.

"My friend Cypher, always humble," Lucas said, smiling as he rolled his eyes. He took my hand and we followed Cypher into the center of the sprawling mess, where a ring of desks circled a clearing. Cypher sat at a chair and pushed himself towards one of the desks surrounded by holo-screens. He started typing at once, his fingers blurring while he… did whatever the hell he was doing.

"Normally I don't like to give him credit," Varsha said as she came to stand next to us. "But for once the annoying idiot is telling the truth. Before Cypher came things were a mess here, but he helped connect the power and rigged solar-generators too for hot water. We have to use these things sparingly, but they brought massive comforts for the people living here."

"Aw shucks, you're going to make me blush!" The bright lights of the terminal illuminated Cypher's face while his fingers rattled over various keyboards. I wondered why anyone would ever need more than one keyboard, but I probably understood less than one percent of what he was doing here.

Eyes on him, I pushed my senses in his direction, trying to see if I could decipher the inner workings of a mind that spoke a language almost unknown to me. This was the one true blessing of my power, emotional states transcended any language barrier, no matter what the tongue.

When I looked in Cypher's mind though, I found something unusual, something I'd never seen before. There was a trace of emotion, and from that I could tell he really did care about these people, and really hated Manucci and everything his oppressive regime represented. The emotion was just a small flake of his mind though, underneath that there was a vast shape, a plane that felt grid-like, highly organized, a million lights all turning off and on in perfect synchronicity, trying to decipher something in front of them.

All of a sudden Cypher's fingers slowed and he turned around in his chair to look at us, confusion evident on his face. "Who's doing that?" he asked, eyeballing us all suspiciously.

"What?" Lucas asked.

"My mind. It felt like... it felt like someone was in there." He looked at me, somehow connecting the dots. "It was you! How did you do that?!"

I stammered, surprised that another person had seen through my powers. "W-Well I'm—"

"She's an empath," Hazel said, stepping forward to answer the question. "How could you tell she was in your mind?"

Cypher looked at the witch and shrugged before turning back to his array of screens, his fingers settling on the keys again. "No idea. I just felt it. My thoughts are highly organized, and I can tell when something is out of place. If you don't mind miss, please stay out of my brain, you're getting in the way of my work."

"Will do. Sorry for intruding. It was impressive by the way. I've never seen anything like it. Your mind is like a computer."

Though we were standing behind him, I saw him smile. "Now I am blushing!"

"God, please don't let his head get any bigger," Varsha said. "He's already insufferable enough. We'll be down in the plaza dork boy. Radio if you have any more visitors."

"Bye wife!" Cypher sang.

"Not your wife," Varsha sang back. She and the other security girls rolled their eyes in a friendly way before leaving. Cypher clearly enjoyed annoying them, but I got the impression everyone was close knit here.

"So what are you working on?" Lucas asked his hacker friend. "You said you've got a way to Manucci, and it involves kidnapping a noble. Which one?"

"That my friend is the question!" Cypher said, lifting his hand theatrically before slamming his forefinger down on the keyboard. He pushed away from his desk, his chair rolling across the floor to a printer on a desk behind him. It started churning and making noise, several sheets of paper firing from inside.

Cypher grabbed them, stood up from his chair and walked over to us, handing out the printouts.

"What are these?" Hazel asked.

"A selection of appropriate targets," Cypher said. "Here you'll find the details of three nobels, all of whom possess tier-two access to Manucci."

"Meaning?" I asked.

"Meaning that they currently work in close proximity to Manucci and have the clearance to meet with him."

"No one knows where Manucci is most of the time," Hazel said. "He's a shadow. He's paranoid."

"And he has every right to be, but you get one of these nobles, and you get Manucci."

"How did you get this information?" Lucas asked Cypher.

"How does a bear catch salmon? With its claws! It's what I was born to do baby! Now quit asking so many questions and listen up. There's a fundraiser tonight at the Asaki Theatre up town. Manucci won't be there, but a bunch of his cronies will be, and I can guarantee one of these nobles will be there too. All you have to do is get in, get the noble, and get out. Once that's done Manucci is as good as yours!"

Lucas, Hazel and I all looked at one another. I had to admit this had the makings of a good plan, one that wasn't without danger.

"We're going to need weapons," Lucas said to Cypher. Cypher just laughed.

"My dear friend Lucas. Do you think I'd send you in there empty-handed? Let me show you my playroom. It's full of sparkly toys and lots of ammo!"

"Who in the hell is this guy," Hazel said as we followed Cypher to his illegal armory.

"I'm just a guy that likes computers and plotting revolution against totalitarian governments. Is that so weird?"

"Yes," we all answered at once.

He chuckled. "Yeah, I suppose it is. Come. Let's get you all stocked and armored. You're going to need some fancy clothes too, and a ride to the theatre. The fundraiser is in a couple of hours. If we hurry we can get everything together in time."

"It's good to be out," Lucas said with a grin.

As I looked at him I couldn't help feel his enthusiasm and thirst for revenge.

It was time for war.

The next few hours were a blur of planning, the four of us dashing about as we prepared for the last minute operation. Cypher's armory made a police station evidence room look like a candy store, and there was also an underground shooting range in the old mall. I'd never actually fired a gun before, but we all went down there and fired a few practice rounds, Lucas showing me the basics of reloading and targeting.

"Now Asaki Theatre is high security," Cypher said, "So we're limited in what you can carry in their weapons wise. I think it's best if you all take the Xenos-11 handguns. They're small and I printed them, so they don't contain enough metal to set off the scanners."

He pulled out a duffel bag and produced a small handgun, probably small enough to fit inside a clutch.

"That thing?" Lucas said with a note of disappointment.

"Hey, you're not going to conceal much more in your tux, and you won't get a rifle past the scanners. You just need something to scare whichever noble you end up abducting." He handed one of the small guns to both of us and offered one to Hazel too.

"What about you witchy?" he said, holding the gun out for her to take it.

"I am a walking gun," Hazel answered. "I don't need one."

"This is Manucci and his goons we're talking about here," Cypher said. "Are you really going to take that chance?"

Hazel looked around at the walls of the gun range, her eyes glistening with contemplation. "How thick would you say the walls are in here? Three feet of concrete?"

"Easily. That's regulation."

Without another word Hazel lifted her hand, pointing her palm at the wall opposite from us. A beam of purple light exploded from her palm and vaporized a hole in the wall, three feet across and three feet deep. We all stared in silent amazement at the smoke pouring from the void.

"Well I'll…" Cypher put the third gun back in the bag and looked at the hole again. "A simple no would have sufficed!"

"What's next?" Lucas asked.

"Costumes and disguises. Varsha has already headed into the city to procure items for the three of you. I took digital biometric scans of your measurements upstairs. Hazel and Olivia, you're both normal, so finding a dress won't be hard, Lucas, you're a freak of nature, so she'd had to stop off at a specialty tailor to find something last minute for your gorilla body."

"You scanned us?" I asked. "Isn't that a violation of our privacy?"

"Coming from the girl that spies on everyone's emotions?" Cypher said with a smirk.

"Touché," I said. I had to admit I was being a little hypocritical there.

"What about disguises?" Lucas. "What did you have in mind?"

A huge grin spread over Cypher's face and I could tell from the glint in his eye he had something special. "Just wait until you see this."

With my crash course firearm training finished we followed Cypher back upstairs to his computer lab, where he produced a crate and set it down on a table in front of us. It was a regular looking milk crate, but the contents were unusual, a pile of semi-transparent rubber masks, paper-thin and quite eerie looking.

"What in the heck are these things?" Lucas said and picked one of the masks up from the crate.

"This!" Cypher said, snatching the mask from Lucas' hands. "Is top-secret military tech, each one of these bad boys is a couple of million, so keep your gorilla hands off until you understand how they work."

"Robbing from the military now? That's an enemy you don't want. Even you."

Cypher waved a dismissive hand. "Those goons? Please. It wasn't even hard to get these, I just hacked into their shipping network and changed a few addresses around. They shipped these things to a PO box for free and I had a courier pick them up!"

"Still Cypher... the military?"

"But look what they can do." Cypher put the mask on and all of a sudden, the loose material sucked onto the contours of his face. In the blink of an eye he looked like someone completely different, a middle-aged Asian man. "Pretty good, huh?! And I can change it too!" He turned to the computer next to him and his fingers blurred over the keyboard. The mask suddenly shifted, turning him into a narrow-faced boy with thick bushy brows.

He hit another button on his keyboard and the mask deactivated, returning back to its original material and peeling off his face.

"Okay I have to admit I'm impressed," Lucas said. "With these things we'll get into the theatre no problem. Half the city is looking for me at the moment."

"That's right, and there's enough for everyone too, so the three of you can slip in and out undetected." He handed a mask to Lucas and me and held one out for Hazel too.

Without saying anything she waved a hand over her face, completely changing her appearance. Cypher put the spare mask back in the box and smiled. "Hey, at least you didn't blow a hole in anything this time!"

"Let's go over the plan a few more times before we have to leave," Lucas said to the group. "We have a little room for error here, a lot can go wrong, and we can't afford that to happen at all."

"We're going to get him," I said with determination. "We can do this."

He smiled at me and nodded. "It's that or death."

LUCAS

Not long after that Cypher's friend, Varsha, returned with the outfits we would be wearing inside the theatre. We all got dressed and met Cypher back in his computer lab before heading up to the roof to leave.

Olivia and Hazel looked like completely different women, both wearing elegant gowns that were fit for royalty. Varsha's tailor had come through for me too, I was now sporting a perfectly cut tuxedo, the sharp finish expertly wrapped around my larger than usual body.

As we stepped onto the roof the whirling blades of a quadrocopter greeted us, gusts of wind blowing in all directions from the powerful turbine engines. We ran into the quadrocopter and all strapped in, Cypher handing us each a headset so we could talk over the noise.

The chopper took off and pulled into the sky, its four engines whirring as we flew forward to our destination.

"I've hacked the vehicle signature so this quadrocopter looks like an envoy vehicle from Manucci's inhouse accountants. The people running his books are basically crooks, glorified money launders."

"Accountants? Really?" I shouted back over the din; our voices barely audible over the quadrocopter.

"Yes, Manucci has thousands of number people on his payroll, they help funnel city funds into his private offshore accounts. No one will blink an eye at you being there. If anyone asks what you do, just say you work in tax. No one ever has any follow up questions, unless they want to fall asleep."

"Hazel and I might get away with looking like accountants, but Lucas? He looks like a professional wrestler!" Olivia pointed out.

"I did think of that," Cypher shouted. "Just say he's your security or something. Chances are you don't have to explain yourself. There are lots of people here, and they're mostly interested in themselves. Just keep your heads down, act normal and find your target. Once you escort them out of the building you just have to call me in and we're out of there."

The rest of the ride we put on our masks, Olivia and I taking on the appearance of completely different people. Hazel changed her face with her magic, going from a brunette with sharp features to a strawberry blonde with a button nose.

I glanced over the profiles of our targets a few more times, we only had to get one to get access to Manucci. There were two men and one woman. My instincts told me it would be easiest to take one of the men, but we could figure out the details on the ground.

After a short ride the quadrocopter finally reached the theatre rooftop, an incoming message playing over the pilot's radio as we approached.

"Incoming chopper, tail number R3D5, identify yourself!" the radio barked.

Cypher's pilot went to answer, but Cypher hijacked his headset. "Hello there niner niner, this is Captain Rodriguez of the..." Cypher grabbed a manifest book on the passenger seat and flicked through it quickly. "4th Air Division, Chapter 3. Carrying three civilians from 'Ashbury Roth Accounting,' requesting permission to land."

There was silence for a few seconds, the tension high as I wondered if we were about to be blown out of the sky.

"Roger that Captain Rodriguez. System flagged you up as suspicious because your vehicle ID came up as fake, I've just refreshed and it's all green here. Bring her down."

"Probably my faulty transponder, damn thing is a pain in the ass! I'll have to put her in the shop!"

"Roger that," the voice from the ground said again. With that Cypher ripped off his headset and closed the laptop that he had just been frantically typing into. "Fuck, that was close. If I hadn't patched our flight ID we would be a heap of flaming wreckage right about now. Last time I trust Zero to get pirated flight IDs for me!"

The quadrocopter touched down on the helipad and we all climbed out, with the exception of Cypher and his pilot. Before we walked away from the quadrocopter Cypher hailed me one last time.

"Remember the plan. Once you have your target signal me and come back to the roof for extraction. No need to sweat this Lucas, you can do this."

I patted Cypher on the shoulder and smiled. "I know I can, I'm just hoping you don't leave us high and dry," I said as I turned to walk away.

"Do I ever?!" he grinned, the quadrocopter firing up its engines again as it took off into the sky. I ran over to Olivia and Hazel who were waiting at the helipad's edge and we headed down the stairs leading into the building. The theatre was a pretty extraordinary looking building, it was twenty stories high and the architecture was both gothic and modern, combining the two ideals in a way that looked strange yet elegant.

Inside the theme continued, sleek black hallways with plush red carpet that led to a bank of silver elevators. A stream of other guests were walking through the hallways, an ocean of elegant upper class elite, most whom had made their money by standing by and enabling Manucci to treat the city like his personal piggybank.

Their pearls and fur suggested class and dignity, but I knew they were just physical manifestations of bribery, little trinkets handed down to yes men that stood by and said nothing while Manucci profited off slavery, racketeering, human trafficking, and worse.

"Okay," Olivia said as she hit the call button for one of the elevators. "The fundraiser is down on the third floor. Let's head down there and start scanning the crowds for our subjects. We all have an earpiece so we can converse without being next to one another."

"And you have me in your ear as well!" Cypher hollered, his voice coming in clear even though he was on a quadrocopter up in the sky.

"I'd like to put my earpiece in the trash please," Hazel quipped. She pushed the button to close the elevator doors before anyone else could get in. They closed, leaving us to talk freely while we rode down to the third floor.

"I'd put my money on the female noble, Sasha Salinsky," Cypher advised. *"She's young blood in Manucci's organization, an up and comer that works his political divisions. Distributing propaganda to make him look good, fielding questions from news agencies that strive to slur Manucci's empire. She's a silver tongue, sharp-minded."*

I shook my head. "No, she's the obvious choice, but I think our best bet is one of the men."

"Really? Why?"

"Honeypot," Olivia said. I nodded at her, she knew exactly what I was talking about.

"Exactly. Olivia and Hazel can bait one of these idiots into straying away from the crowd. Once that's done, all I have to do is show up and look menacing. It's plain-sailing."

"I hadn't thought of that, it's brilliant! It's just a question of who you target now. There's an old guy and a young guy. The young guy is a weapon's dealer for Manucci, the older one works in finance. I guess it all comes down to which guy you think would be easier to honeypot—"

"Old guy," Olivia and Hazel answered at once, giving each other a knowing glance.

The doors dinged open, revealing a grand and sprawling room filled with thousands of attendees. From the attire alone it was clear this was an exclusive event, a social soiree only for the highest of society. Elaborate ballgowns, sparkling jewelry, fat men in tops and tails, tweaking their monocles and blowing cigar smoke up towards the glittering chandeliers overhead.

Olivia and I both stepped forward to leave the elevator when

Hazel stuck her arm out and stopped us. "Wait," she said, a sense of dread evident on her face.

"Hazel? What's wrong?" Olivia asked.

"Something isn't right here. I can feel it." Hazel took an uncertain step forward, her eyes growing glassy as she stared across the vast ball room, scanning the crowds for some unknown entity. She's stopped and nodded slightly at something imperceptible. "That's it."

"What?" I asked, my body suddenly jumping to high-alert, wondering if we should run back to the elevator and signal for extraction straight away.

"It's my sister, Zaya. She's here somewhere, I can feel her. I think she just realized that I'm here too." Hazel then pulled something out of the clutch bag making up her outfit, it was a small glass stone, faintly glowing with dim light. She crushed the stone in her palm, and it dissolved, the faint light dissipating into her arm.

"Aw fuck," Cypher cursed over the radio. *"All right guys, I'm calling it. Mission cancelled. Head back up to the roof for immediate extraction. We are not prepared for a witch showdown."*

"No," Hazel said dismissively. "It's too late. She already knows I'm here. Leaving now will only delay the inevitable. There's no getting away now, one way or another we have to fight."

"Not ideal," I reminded her.

"It's unavoidable. There's nothing I can do. I'll keep us hidden for as long as I can and try to buy you guys time, but I can't promise much."

"What do we do?" Olivia asked. "How do we help?"

"Get out into the crowd and find our old guy. I'll keep my distance on the other side of the room, keeping Zaya's attention away from you."

Olivia and I looked at one another, swallowed down our nerves and walked forward. I took her hand and glanced back at Hazel as we slipped into the crowd, our eyes searching all around as we looked for our target. I took Olivia's hand and hoped Hazel could give us enough time to find our guy before all hell broke loose.

A twisting stomach in my feeling had me on edge though. Something big was about to happen. We had to move fast.

———

"Not to hurry you guys, but have you found the target yet or what?!" Cypher droned in our ears.

"No we haven't," I whispered under my breath. "I'm not sure if you noticed how many people there are in here, but we're looking for a needle in a haystack. There are literally thousands of fat cats in suits."

"Well I have noticed, because I hacked the surveillance cameras and I'm watching everything as we speak. Let me see if I can dig a little deeper on this old guy and find some clues."

Olivia and I both smiled at a middle-aged couple passing our way, the man and woman giving us a slightly wide birth while looking me up and down. They weren't the only ones that had looked at me funny so far. Quite a lot of eyes were coming my way, including those of the security guards at the edge of the room.

"Relax," Olivia said, clearly picking up on my worrying. "They don't suspect anything; they're just intrigued mostly. It's not everyday people see someone as big as you."

"What else are you picking up from the crowds? Anything useful?"

"A lot of ego and a lot of insecurity. It is *not* fun being in these people's heads. How can someone be so rich and so afraid at the same time?"

"Comes with the territory," Cypher said. *"Love to look down on the little guy, hate to think they've not got as much as the bigger guy. Classic rich person problem. Nothing is ever enough. Humans are greedy... speaking of greedy!"*

Silence beat over the comms for a second, prompting Olivia and I to look at one another in confusion while we waited for Cypher to speak. We couldn't very well keep muttering under our breath unless we wanted to look crazy, so we had to speak sparingly.

"Cypher?" I prompted.

"Sorry! I got distracted reading. I think I might know where our guy is.

Herman Bass, one of the early backers of Manucci's political campaign. He's fourth generation wealth, born rich and never worked to earn it, but greases the palms of fucks like Manucci to make sure his money keeps growing."

"That's great, but do you have a position on him?"

"I ran face-search on the crowd but it's not pulling up anything. That either means he's not in here or..."

"Or his face isn't visible?"

"Bingo! I found something here that says Bass is a big food lover. Apparently this guy owns like a third of all the restaurants in Carcoza city. Did you guys check out the buffet?"

We hadn't. Circling around Olivia and I started working our way through the crowd, moving in the direction of the giant buffet table that almost took up the entire length of the back wall. Bass wasn't a conventional looking type, he had shaggy black hair that was kind of messy, and the photo on his file suggested he was bigger around the midriff.

"There!" Olivia said excitedly, quickly stifling her energy so not to arouse suspicion. She subtly pointed across the crowd to a man with shoulder-length shaggy black hair, a large plate in his hand as he wolfed down a mountain of appetizers. No wonder Cypher's facial recognition scan couldn't find the guy, he was eating like a pig in a trough.

Excellent.

"Bonus fact," Cypher said, *"This will probably help with your honeypot scheme, Bass is recently divorced, so he's single and ready to mingle."*

"Looks like the mingling has already begun," I said, noting a bored-looking blonde escort who was stood just off to the side of Bass, eyeballing the rest of the crowd, looking like she'd rather be anywhere else. "He has a date, though I can't say she looks thrilled about it."

"She's not," Olivia said, her eyes focused in a way that told me she was reading the girl. "But it's work, nonetheless. She's getting paid good money for this. Ooh, she's noticed us approaching, or you specifically. She likes what she sees. We could use this."

The skinny blonde suddenly perked up, her eyes lighting with life as she looked in my direction. Olivia and I were walking in their direction at a steady pace, acting as if we were simply scanning the long table of food for choice.

"Too bad I'm taken," I said.

"Not right now you're not." Olivia pushed me forward a step while she pretended to veer off and study something at the buffet. "You pull her away from him and I'll move in."

"What?" I said, surprised that Olivia was even suggesting this.

"Go! I'm not jealous!"

I carried on walking, passing Bass and his date only to stop a few paces behind them, bending down as I pretended to tie my shoe. His date turned around not so subtly as she tried to find me, stopping as she saw me stand up again. I nodded at her and then tilted my head in the direction of the bathrooms. Her eyes widened and she nodded back.

Turning around I walked over to the bathrooms, the crowds thinning again as I reached the edge of the room. I saw the escort come my way, and as soon as she was gone Olivia slipped into Bass's side, pretending to trip and fall on him. I couldn't help smiling as I watched her. She was good, there was no denying it.

"So what did you have in mind big boy?" the blonde said as she came up to me. "I'm technically working, but I can probably fit you in for a quick consultation."

I looked at the girl, my eyes flaring with the power of my vampiric intention. "You're going to go home and get a good night's sleep. When you wake up tomorrow you won't remember anything about this night. You're getting tired now."

The blonde let out a long yawn. "Let's take a rain check, tiny. I'm getting tired now. I better tell Herman—" she turned to head back in his direction when I flared my control again.

"Forget the old man. You just want to go home."

"Ah, fuck him," she said. "All he cares about is food anyway." With that the blonde disappeared into the crowds, heading in the direction of the exit. I made my way back to Olivia and our target, delighted to see Herman throwing his head back and roaring with laughter as Olivia worked him over.

"He's here now actually," I heard her say, gesturing for me to come over. "Dr. Cooper, over here!"

I went over, smiling at them both on the approach. "Dr. Taylor," I said. "Schmoozing men again?"

Olivia laughed. "I was just telling the fine Mr. Bass here about our work with lab-grown meat and how we just had our first million-dollar order. It's big profit for everyone, especially the vendors selling to consumers!"

"Who was it?!" Herman said excitedly as he took a big chunk out of a chicken leg. "Chang? I bet you sold to Chang, that slimy little fuck is always trying to get ahead of me! Well let me tell you something, my checkbook is bigger, and my restaurants are better reviewed! Why don't the three of us go somewhere and talk? I'd be very delighted to know you better Miss Taylor."

I was surprised at how easy this was, but then I remembered who I was with. Not only could Olivia read this guy's deepest darkest desires, she'd clearly tapped into his biggest insecurities straightaway, twisting them to manipulate him. Part of me expected we would have to use Olivia as bait to pull Herman away from the crowds, but Olivia had done one better.

The fastest way to a man's heart—his stomach.

"Let me put this on the table, I'll be right back!" Herman said, waddling excitedly as he made his way over to the buffet table.

"I have to admit," I said to Olivia under my breath, "this is easier than I anticipated."

"I interrogate serial killers for a living, wrapping this guy around my finger is child's play. I could do it in my sleep. He only has two things on his mind, food and money. I knew the seductive act wouldn't work. The only reason he had an escort was to keep other gold diggers away from him. He wanted to eat in peace!"

"Only one thing better than the taste of food. The taste of profit."

"Olivia, I have to say I'm impressed!" Cypher said. "This is next-level social interrogation!"

"What can I say," she said with a casual shrug. "It's what I do."

Herman came back to us, looking out of breath just from the short trip to the table and back. "I have an office set aside on the fifth floor, let's go talk in there. I can have the staff bring up more food."

"Actually I was hoping you might come to our HQ and check out the supply line. We can put on a spread there, and I think you might like what you see."

"No, we stay here," Herman said flippantly. It was the tone of a man used to getting his way and never hearing the word no. "It's quicker, and I'm getting hungry. Let's go upstairs. You can tell me more about the profit margins on the way."

Olivia and I gave one another an unsure glance but followed Herman anyway. Maybe this wouldn't be as straightforward as I assumed.

"It's fine!" Cypher said, his voice ever-present in our ears. *"Once you have him in the elevator you bring out the guns and ride to the top floor. I can bring in the chopper now and you can get out of there!"*

"What about Hazel?" Olivia muttered under her breath.

"What?!" Herman shouted at Olivia. He was droning on about his restaurant empire and neither of us were really listening.

"Uh, Hazel, that new restaurant in the center. I heard it had rave reviews. Is that one of yours?"

Herman's fat pudgy face wrinkled like a confused prune. "You know I think it is actually, it's hard to keep up these days, anyway—"

"Hazel said to get the target and get out. She has to keep her sister distracted. I've not heard anything from her, but hey, we've seen what she can do, she can take care of herself. The good news is the mission is as good as done, now get this fat slob up to the roof and—"

Whatever Cypher was going to say we didn't hear it.

Just then a huge explosion tore through the ballroom, an orb of crackling white light that knocked everyone in the room to their feet. My instincts took over and I immediately dived for Olivia, disregarding Herman completely.

In the ensuing seconds chaos was everywhere. The crowds jumped to their feet and started screaming, people running for the exits in every direction while the fire alarms blared loudly, spraying water across the room. Olivia and I stood up and looked in the direction of the explosion, seeing a woman with long white hair floating in the middle of the room, gusts of winds billowing all around her.

Standing across from her was Hazel, her body also charged with crackling waves of her magical power.

"So good to see you again, sister!" the dark-witch announced loudly, her voice somehow filling the room from all sides. "And you brought your friends with you. I must admit you saved me a job!"

Now the room was almost empty, only a few hundred people left as they scrambled for the exits. Looking around at the many doors leading out of the room I saw vampires step in at every entrance, closing the doors behind them. Manucci's men. There had to be at least twenty of them, two at every door.

"Uh guys, not to make you panic or anything, but I think we may have been compromised!" Cypher said over our in-ear radio.

"Compromised?" another voice said, echoing over loud-speakers from somewhere within the room. Then I saw a figure emerge on the stage at the opposite end of the room, safely behind the floating dark witch.

It was Manucci.

"You slipped up the second you landed on the roof of this theatre!" Manucci barked. "My security flagged it up, and my good assistant Zaya here detected an old familiar presence. Speaking of old and familiar… how are you doing Lucas?!"

With our cover blow I ripped Cypher's face-changing mask from my face. Olivia followed suit. "I'm good. Ready to kill you and have this done with."

Manucci threw his head back and laughed. "Look around you Lucas! You're outnumbered and outgunned. Your witch friend is no match for her sister, and you can't fight off my men while protecting your little pet!"

"Just watch me," I growled.

He faked a yawn. "Whatever. I'm bored of this. Kill the witch and kill the traitor. Keep the girl alive. Someone bring her to me when this is all done."

Rage boiling in my blood, I watched as Manucci disappeared off the stage again, leaving us to this showdown with his men. Things exploded with the dark witch attacking first, a beam of black light tore from her hands, swallowing Hazel in a ball of roaring black fire.

"Prepare to die!" the dark witch cackled. I grabbed Olivia and saw Manucci's men advancing.

I had to think of something.

Fast.

LUCAS

"*L*ucas! What do we do?!" Olivia said in a panic. Manucci's men lifted their guns and opened fire, countless bullets streaming towards us from all directions. My rage exploded at once, coursing through my body in a sub-second reaction that tore my neatly tailored suit into shreds.

Cypher had given us both a number of gadgets to help infiltrate Manucci's manor when we got there, but seeing as that plan had changed now I decided to deploy some toys. Though Olivia and I had the appearance of fancy partygoers on the outside we were both wearing bulletproof vests and our outfits concealed a number of devices, Cypher having primed us on them before the mission.

"Olivia, cover, now!" I shouted, pounding my fist against my chest and hers to activate a invisibility cloak that would last for a minute. My speed and strength heightened, I grabbed Olivia and jumped, shooting up from the floor and towards the decorated ceilings high above us, landing in one of the giant chandeliers that overlooked the room.

Temporarily invisible, we had cover to put together a quick plan, and a perfect view of the floor below. The room was a giant square, and on the north side the two witches ripped around the air at lightning speed, blasting each other with brightly colored bolts of deathly magic. On the southside the guards charging at us all came to a stop and looked around in confusion to see us gone.

"What are you thinking?!" Olivia panted, her hands trembling as she held her gun.

"I'm thinking we're in a tricky situation. Cypher what do you think?" I waited, but there was no answer. "Cypher?! Damn it. He must have closed the connection for privacy. Well that's him out."

I looked back down at the guards below us. On my own I could probably take them, but with Olivia here I couldn't risk her getting hurt. There had to be something I could do. Looking up at the ceiling I noticed a square section that looked like it could be pushed up.

"You. Up there," I said.

"Fine, but let me gift you this first. Grab me when the guards are gone. I have a plan for Zaya." Unexpectedly she reached up her dress and pulled something out—a plasma grenade.

"Where the hell did you get that?!"

"Cypher's armory. Varsha gave it to me. She said every girl should carry a surprise up her dress."

"I don't even know what that means, but this is definitely helpful. Get up there and hide. Go!" I kissed her and helped Olivia up into the secret panel. Once she was gone I clicked the button on the side of the plasma grenade and let it cook for a few seconds, the small neon blue device beeping to let me know the explosion was imminent.

My hand hovering over the side of the chandelier, I let go of the grenade and watched as it fell towards the ground. The men below only noticed it right at the last moment, just as it bounced off the rug at the center of their group.

"Grenad—!" one began to shout, his words vaporized as the bright explosion tore through the majority of the group. Just as my invisibility cloak faded, I dropped from the sky like death above. Three of the group were still alive.

Not for long.

The first died as I hit the ground and plunged a dagger through the back of his neck. His two colleagues were both still reeling from the explosion, giving me time to flash forwards across the floor and gut them both too.

As the last one died, I pulled my blade out, blood spraying out in a fine arc of mist. The guard hit the ground and burst into fire and flame. For a second there was the quietude of victory, but it didn't last long.

"Look out!" a voice shouted my way, it was Hazel. I didn't have time to look back, I just jumped into the air and launched backwards, throwing myself into a backflip to launch over whatever threat was coming my way.

As I flew through the air, I saw it, time slowing down in my adrenaline-heightened state. A huge beam of magical energy scorched through the air, absolutely demolishing the ground where I had just been standing. Zaya and Hazel quickly followed after, both tangled together as furious balls of violent magic, going at each other with everything they had.

Landing back on the floor I found my breath and looked up at the ceiling to see Olivia had pulled back the panel. "Get me down!" she said. "I can stop this!"

Olivia was strong, I knew as much, but even I had no idea how she was going to stop a witch fight. Hazel and her hypnotized sister were absolutely tearing this room to shreds, throwing one another around with so much power that I knew there was nothing *I* could do to stop it.

Somehow though I knew Olivia could solve this. If anyone could, it would be her.

With another powerful jump I vaulted up to the chandelier and helped Olivia climb onto the light with me. "So, what's this plan?"

"If I can just talk to her I can stop her," she said. "I'm sure. I saw something when I looked inside the mind of the Drowga. A vision about Zaya. Something about a necklace."

The two of us watched helplessly as both witches blasted around the room as tornadoes of magical death, entwined in a fight that could vaporize a mortal in seconds. Gusts of violent wind and stray blasts of magical light exploded in every direction. We weren't safe even all the way up here.

Just then a high-pitched whistling formed in our ear. We both winced and held our earpieces. The frequency was unbearably loud and went on for a few seconds, so uncomfortable that it even made the witches pause.

Sure enough it ended and the fight resumed again, almost instantly.

"Sorry!" Cypher's voice said over the comms. *"That was me. I had to establish a new connection on a private channel. Manucci was listening on the other one, but now we have total privacy. I see you guys are still alive! Well done!"*

"Yeah, not for much longer though. If we don't contain this fight soon the entire city will be levelled. Any gadgets to take out feuding witches?"

Cypher laughed. *"Even I have my limits, Lucas, geez! If you guys have any ideas, I might be able to help though!"*

"The frequency," Olivia said. "Hazel and Zaya both paused then when that audio interference broke through the air. Cypher, can you fill this room with a high-pitched sound, maybe for thirty seconds?"

"Easily! All I have to do is ramp up the amp feedback through the sound system and—" Suddenly one of the stray blasts of magical light came our way and eviscerated the chandelier, meaning that Olivia and I found ourselves plummeting right into the path of the dueling witches. I grabbed her and screamed at Cypher to act.

"Just do it!" I yelled, preparing to throw myself in front of any magic that might harm Olivia.

As soon as we hit the ground the high-pitched frequency exploded, ripping through the air as a blast of shrill sound, so uncomfortable that I had to cover my ears. Both Hazel and Zaya dropped to the ground, their hands clamped over their heads as they wailed in agony.

Olivia ran over to the dark witch without hesitating, crouching down in front of her and putting a hand on her shoulder, she leaned in close, so close that her mouth was right against the dark witch's ear, and she shouted something over the din.

Just as the shrill sound stopped playing I heard Olivia's voice loud and clear.

"…he gave something to you, didn't he? He told you he loved you. He said it was a gift. What was it?"

Both Hazel and I watched, frozen in terror as Olivia talked to the dark witch. The platinum-haired woman was still on the ground, curled up in a ball as she listened to Olivia. I think we were both waiting for her to resume her attack, but she didn't. She actually… she actually talked back to Olivia.

"He said it was special. A family heirloom." Zaya sat up, tears streaming down her face, and pulled a necklace out from her robes. It was a strange looking thing, a heart amulet made of dark black metal, veins of purple magic throbbing over its surface.

Olivia took one look at the necklace and nodded her head. "You know what I am, don't you? An empath. I can see inside people. I can see the things that make them tick. You never loved him before this amulet, did you? Do you remember?"

Zaya shook her head. "No, I always loved him."

Olivia shook her head. "No, you didn't, and you don't. He trapped you with this. It's the thing controlling you. I saw it in your mind when I looked in the Drowga. I saw it in Manucci's mind when he was on that stage. This is it Zaya. This is the thing keeping you imprisoned. Let me take it off. Let me set you free."

She reached forward to grab the amulet. I half-expected the witch to recoil or explode into combat again, but she didn't. Olivia took the amulet off and then… a change came over the dark witch instantly.

All at once she sat up straight, her body no longer sinking under the oppressive weight of Manucci's control and his strange magical device. Zaya blinked, looking around the room like someone waking from a very long sleep.

She laughed and then she stood up, Olivia mirroring the action.

"Zaya," Hazel said cautiously. "Are you okay?"

"Oh, I'm more than okay sister. A little annoyed that bastard had me under his control for so long, but hey… it was my fault for putting the damn amulet on in the first place. I got greedy. He told me it would make me powerful. If you'll all excuse me for a moment."

Zaya disappeared in a flash of light. She was only gone for a few seconds, but in that absence Hazel, Olivia and I looked at each other in confusion.

Then the witch returned, a bolt of supersonic white light that came to a stop just in front of us. She threw Manucci onto the ground in front of me. He hit the floor like a sack of shit, scrambling to his knees and looking around in terror.

"Lucas! Wait, we can talk! I can make you powerful! I can give you everything!"

I looked past his groveling and focused on the dark witch standing just behind him. "Just admit it," I said. "You framed me for those murders. Why?"

"I had to Lucas! You were going to get the mayorship! God, can you imagine what a shithole this city would be if you'd won! I had to lock you away, it was for your own good!"

"You get that Cypher?" I said into my ear.

"Crystal clear, saving the surveillance footage as we speak!"

Zaya eyed me. "Are you killing him or what?"

"You do it. He took your life."

"You're sure?" she asked. "Vengeance is the one thing I want, but I know your story too. I know what he did to you. Don't you want this?"

My eyes moved to Olivia, who was standing at my side. I glanced back at Zaya and shook my head. "No. Not anymore. I got everything I wanted. He's yours now. I've got a city to fix."

"Lucas wait!" Manucci groveled as I took Olivia's hand and started walking away. "You can't leave me here alone with her! She'll kill me! Lucas! Lucas!"

We reached the exit just as an explosion of light flashed behind us, silencing Manucci immediately. Glancing back I saw his lifeless body on the ground, and I knew that it was finally done.

Manucci was dead, Zaya was free, and I had Olivia at my side.

It was time to start anew.

EPILOGUE - OLIVIA

As we came out of the courthouse we were met with a sea of flashing cameras, hundreds of reporters all shouting our names, scrambling to get the first word from Lucas now that he was free and officially found innocent.

After Manucci fell his entire organization started crumbling, a giant house of cards that turned to dust in a moment. With unfettered access to the inner workings of the empire, Cypher was able to find the evidence proving that Manucci was actually the one guilty of all those murders. Lucas was proven innocent and now as he walked out of the courthouse I was at his side, ready to take on this new world with him.

We stopped at a press podium that had been put aside for us, basking for a moment in the energy coming from the crowd of clamoring people below us.

"Lucas, Lucas! Is it true you weren't the one to kill Manucci?!"

"Lucas, any word on the rumors of you running for office?!"

"Olivia, do you plan on sticking around?!"

Question after question blasted through the air, Lucas and I looking at one another in quiet excitement as we prepared ourselves.

Lucas approached the stand and leaned into the microphone, gesturing for everyone to quiet down so he could speak.

"Okay, everyone quiet down. We'll answer a few questions, but I'm not going to stay here long. I've got work to do. We've got work to do." He looked at me and smiled, pointing at a reporter near the front as everyone started shouting for his attention again. Everyone quietened down and the reporter spoke up.

"Are you surprised by the surge of support following Manucci's death? It seems like most of the city was rooting for you all along, hoping you might take control again one day."

"The support has been brilliant," Lucas said. "I couldn't ask for more. Right now I'm just acting in a voluntarily capacity until the seat of power officially transitions over. We want to do things the right way and ensure something like this can never happen again. Leaders will have terms; people will be given an opportunity to have a future that benefits them."

The reporters all broke out in a serious of frenzied questions as Lucas's answer came to an end. He quickly pointed at another reporter, drawing the crowd into silence.

"What about the calls for a complete change of the system?" A young man with glasses asked. "A group of people out there, and not a small group, are saying the mayorship should be abolished all together. They want Carcoza as an independent territory, a country where vampires can live free, side-by-side with humans!"

Lucas chuckled at the suggestion. "I have heard the voice, and as you said it is not a small one. If the vampire people want a country of their own, that is something that will have to be established with the American government. A change of that size, it could benefit vampire and humankind greatly, but things would drastically differ. There would be more positions of power for instance, a president above a mayor, and so forth."

Once again, the clamor of questions broke forth again, but the glasses-wearing reporter continued. "No, you're mistaken. The people of Carcoza aren't asking for a vampire president. They want a monarchy, a man and woman that can lead our people forward indefinitely!"

A look of confusion came over Lucas's face, we both glanced at one another. Reading the energy from the group in front of us I could feel something brewing, a great tide of hope and unity that was shared amongst each and every person.

"I uh… haven't heard anything about that," Lucas said. "You're proposing we elect a king and queen?"

"Not just any king and queen!" Another reported shouted. "You! The people want you. Lucas and Olivia!"

All at once the crowd roared in unison, and Lucas and I found ourselves staring at one another in utter bewilderment. If I didn't know any better, I'd think I was dreaming, but I was hearing was really true, the people of the city wanted a king and queen to lead them forward, and they were calling on *us!*

"Well—" Lucas began, faltering as he tried to find the words for the flattering proposal.

"Well you've certainly given us something to think about!" I said through laughter. "I guess we'll see what happens going forward. If the people want leadership, then they will get it!"

Another roar of approval met my words, and a surge of adrenaline rushed through me as I heard the cheering. For the first time since coming here I felt hope in the air, like the shackles of despair were finally starting to lift and give life to a new dawn.

"Does that mean we can expect a wedding?" a young female reporter shouted from the crowd. "If a king has a queen then that implies marriage? Does Lucas Vancino believe he has found that woman?"

The question was met with an excited sweep of sound, mostly from the other female reporters. Everyone looked at Lucas in expectation. He smiled at the question and glanced at me.

"When I first met Olivia, I knew straightaway that she was different. I don't have to look very far. I've already found my queen."

Without another word he pulled me in and kissed me deeply, the crowd exploding in a wall of excited cheering and hollering. We pulled away from one another and my heart was beating in my chest, my head dizzy from euphoria.

"I guess that means I've found my vampire king then," I whispered to him through my smile.

"Vampire king?" he said with a questioning brow. "I like the sound of that. I guess that makes you my vampire queen?"

"Why don't we get out of here and head home? I think the king and queen need to celebrate in private."

Lucas grinned and took my hand, lifting it to wave as we left the stage and said our goodbyes to the crowd.

Coming here I thought this city would be the end of me. Now I realize it was just the beginning. I had a king, a savior, a man that loved me, and a man that would fight for the future of this city.

I was his queen; he was my king. This city was our kingdom.

I wouldn't have it any other way.

THANKS FOR READING

Thanks for reading!

It would mean the world to me if you could leave an honest review for this book, every review helps me out. :)

Blood Lust

MAILING LIST

Join my mailing list to stay up to date. It's for new releases only, no
spam:
http://eepurl.com/b5tmt5

Follow me on Facebook for updates and general chatter:
https://www.facebook.com/TalesOfVampires

Or just drop me an email:
redlotuspublishing@gmail.com